The Ancient

An Anthology By

The Seven

Copyright © 2015 The Seven, Loni Townsend, Marlie Harris,
Sherry Briscoe, Rochelle Cunningham, Catherine Valenti, Bobbi
Carol, Troy Lambert

All rights reserved.

ISBN: **1508550859**
ISBN-13: **978-1508550853**

INTRODUCTION

Under a tent at Garibaldi Days, Sherry Briscoe looked at me, and said the words: I have an idea. The Seven was born. Like all of our children-ideas, it went through some growing pains, and some transformations, but here is its debut: a group of Seven authors writing in their own genre about one thing: The Ancient.

The Rules were simple really. Write about a lamp, or something like a lamp, the ancient power of those who can grant wishes. Thus we found the common theme: be careful what you wish for.

Join us, The Seven, on our journey into the world of The Ancient.

.

CONTENTS

	Acknowledgments	i
	Introduction	ii
1	Smokeless Flame	1
2	The Golden Pen	Pg 21
3	A Lauder Way	Pg 39
4	A Wish to Give	Pg 57
5	Lily and the Lamp	Pg 73
6	Reaction	Pg 97
7	The Multiplier	Pg 1119

ACKNOWLEDGMENTS

A thanks to Sherry Briscoe for being the idea girl, Rochelle Cunningham for being the note taker, Cathy Valenti, Marlie Harris, and Bobbi Carol for your proofreading and editing skills, and to our critique partners, life partners, and the others who support us. As always, a big thanks to Elle Rossi for a gorgeous cover.

Most of all, we thank you, the reader, for picking up this little collection and giving it a chance.

SMOKELESS FLAME

Loni Townsend

No smoke. No flicker. The flame just vanished, swallowed by darkness.

Jensen struck another match. White-orange flame flashed to life with a flurry of sparks. Heat flared at her fingertips, carrying with it a whiff of sulfur. She moved it toward the candle. Again, it disappeared.

"Having trouble?" The voice rang with cold derision, though not enough to ruffle her feathers.

She offered the darkness a tight-lipped smile and tried a third match. This one stayed lit, and bright flame caught the candlewick. It danced on the end. Happy to be alive? Or mocking her past failed attempts?

Chang pushed past her into the cavern. "Next time, I'll add lighting candles to the job requirements."

She cupped her hand around the flame, making sure his hot air didn't extinguish her hard work.

Marco stopped at her side with a handful of candlesticks and lit them off hers. "Go easy on her," he said to Chang. "At least she brought the candles."

Chang snorted. "Preparation doesn't equal competence. The next time you hire someone, check their qualifications better."

Marco's brow furrowed, making the scar above his eyebrow turn white. "But I didn't…" He sighed, shook his head, and leaned close to Jensen. "You're doing great for your first day."

She smirked.

Beth materialized from the tunnel shadows. She pushed her glasses up the bridge of her nose, and alternated between mashing the blue and yellow buttons on the device in her hand. "Don't know why the flashlights aren't working in here. Think it's too cold? No, not much colder in here than the tunnel. Give me one of those, will you?"

Marco handed her a candle, and then handed two to Lawrence, the last crew member, and a gangly boy.

Jensen hung back as the others spread out into the cavern. Stone curved in a dome over their heads. It was far too perfect to be natural. Too perfect to be man-made either. Why would something like this be inside the mountain? "This place doesn't belong here."

Dark shadows splayed across the sandy floor, stretching from the people who held lights. She dug the toe of her boot into the yellow grains. *Desert* sand. Where had it come from? Unintelligible murmurs echoed from deeper in the shadows. Someone moved at the corner of her vision. She turned to look. No one.

"Found something." Beth lifted her candle. "Bring the other candles. I need more light. Careful, the footing's uneven over here."

Jensen hiked her bag further up her shoulder and moved closer. Sand slid out from beneath her soles. She pitched sideways and hopped a couple times to regain her balance.

Wiry fingers wrapped around her bicep and dug into her bare flesh. Lawrence's long face leaned close. Mint-tinted breath washed over her cheek. "You okay?"

She nodded. "Thank you."

He unwound his hand and shoved it into his parka's pocket, while his other hand clutched the pair of precariously tipped candles. "How are you not cold?"

"Lawrence!" Chang shouted. "Stop flapping your gums. We're waiting."

The boy jerked and turned back to his original task. His

abrupt movement blew out his candles.

"Clumsy oaf." A Chang-shaped shadow stomped toward them. "Give me th—"

The shadow face-planted. Marco's rich chuckle reverberated through the cavern, and a quick snort came from Beth's location. Jensen bit her lip, but not before Chang's scarlet, sand-speckled face turned its glare on her. She hastily averted her gaze and focused on relighting Lawrence's candles.

Chang got up and dusted himself off without comment, while she and Lawrence carried their light toward Beth's discovery.

Bronze shone in the ruddy glow. Beth rubbed the surface clean with her fingers. "It looks like one of those old oil lamps." Candlelight cast the lamp's reflection in her glasses. "Plain, no jewels or anything. There might be some writing though."

Jensen leaned closer and extended a hand. "May I see it?"

Beth ignored her and pulled the lamp closer to her face. "Hard to tell anything in this weak light." Fire blazed in the background of the reflection, too large to be the candle's flame. "I wish our flashlights were working."

Wind howled through the passage they'd entered, extinguishing candles and plunging them into darkness. Sand pelted the back of Jensen's neck and arms. She hunched against the assault.

"Eep!" Lawrence twisted wildly before going down. He latched onto the closest thing he found—her ankle—and yanked it out from under her. Her supply bag struck the ground first, and she landed hard on top of it. Something cracked and moisture saturated her back.

The blast subsided into an exaggerated breeze. Thin strips of yellow light stretched across the ceiling and wall. Beth clambered to her toppled bag. She pulled out a flashlight and waved it around the space. "Looks like we've got power. Marco, mind taking this? I want to check the rest of the equipment." She lifted the lamp over her head.

Marco stepped gingerly over strewn supplies and took charge of the cavern's treasure. He nestled it beneath his arm. "Anyone hurt?"

The others muttered variations of no. Jensen winced. "I think I broke something."

Lawrence patted her arms and shoulders before groping too far and catching her breast. He jerked his hand back. "Sorry. What'd you break?"

"Water bottle." She sat up and shrugged off her pack. Her braid tangled in one of the straps, and it took some finagling to unwind it. The bag sloshed and she grimaced. "A couple maybe."

Chang sighed and grabbed the bag from her. "Let me take a look." He pawed through the contents. "A third of our water supply, gone. We'll replace the broken canteens back at the campsite."

Air touched Jensen's soaked shirt and goose bumps rippled down her arms. A shiver coursed through her. If it weren't for the water... "Beth, do you have a spare shirt?"

Beth tugged a long-sleeved thermal from a side pocket and tossed it to her. "This is probably too big for your skinny ass, but should keep you warm. Want a coat too?"

"No." Jensen turned her back to the group and pulled the wet shirt off. She wrung the water from it before dropping it in the sand at her feet.

A cone of light cast her silhouette against the cavern wall.

"Interesting choice of tattoos," Chang said from behind her. "What are those supposed to be? Angel wings?"

She rolled her eyes. Guess his mother never taught him to respect a woman's privacy. "Do you have proof angels have wings?"

"Not sure angels even exist." His footsteps crunched closer. "Unless you're one?"

Marco snorted. "That is the *worst* pick-up line I've ever heard."

Lawrence and Beth shared a chuckle. Jensen slid the new shirt on and pulled it down. It hung to her thighs and didn't hug her curves like it did Beth's. But then, the other woman had more to offer.

Jensen ran a hand beneath her braid and extended her arm until the hair slipped free of the neck hole and dropped down her back. It slapped her tailbone through her moleskin trousers. Then she shielded her eyes with a hand and spun to face Chang and his flashlight. "Angel wings are purely a human conjecture. Seraphim have six wings, Cherubim have four, and there is nothing that says either of those beings are actually angels."

Chang dropped the light beam. It sniffed at his toes like a hound no longer interested in its master's prey. Hopefully it would pee on him. "That's the most you've said at one time. Where's your accent from?"

She stooped to retrieve her shirt and shook the sand from the frozen cloth. "The mountains."

"That's unspecific. We deal in details here. Try again."

She stared at her shirt, rubbing the cloth between her fingers. Ice crystals flaked off. "Northern Himalayas, west tip of China." She snapped it in the air before rolling it into a neat bundle.

He folded his arms, and the flashlight beam swung across the sand. Now the hound was prowling. "Himalayans aren't blonde."

"Mister Chang." Marco stepped up, his smile one of exaggerated patience. "I'm sure we'll have time to harass our newest addition tonight. Perhaps we should search for artifacts before another blast comes and buries us?" He held out the lamp.

Chang glowered at Marco, but took his attention off Jensen long enough for her to mouth 'thank you'. She squinted at the lamp and reached out. "May I—"

"Give me that." Chang snatched the lamp from Marco's hand. "I'm going to box this. If I leave it to someone else, it'll probably get ruined." He pulled out a small crate from his bag, laid the lamp inside, and then returned it to his bag. "Let's tie down the rest of the equipment in case the wind rises again."

Jensen sighed as the zipper closed.

Marco set his bag next to Jensen's and bit down on his flashlight to free up his hands. He pulled out a rope and lifted his gaze. His flashlight lit the cavern wall. A face grinned down at them. Ivory teeth gleamed within dark skin. Gold eyes glinted.

Marco tensed and grabbed the light from between his teeth. "There are pictures painted on the walls."

Jensen studied the image. Vibrant cloth twisted around the man's head, and a white plume extended from a glittering amulet fixed in the center of his forehead. Her stomach tightened as she read the text scratched into the wall. *Magician*.

"Hey guys, check it out!" Lawrence pointed his flashlight at the center of the dome's ceiling. "That's a big bird." Gold feathers spread across the diameter of the dome. Massive talons splayed wide, and the painted beak hung open in a silent screech. "What kind do you think it is?"

Jensen struck a match and relit her candle. "It's a roc."

He frowned. "I've never heard of them. Is it from the same family as the eagle?"

Beth laid her bag next to theirs. "Eagles exist. Giant mythical birds do not."

Lawrence's flashlight beam slid along the wingspan. "Oh. Are you sure it's a roc then?"

Jensen smiled and bent to gather dropped candles. "Pretty sure."

He stepped backward, his flashlight lighting a scene of a young man in a hole, and a lamp under his arm. "I guess that explains the—" Something snapped. His light darted to his boots. "Eiii! It's a body!"

He fell backwards, this time without the aid of wind. The yellow flashlight beam made awkward retreating hops as he crab-scrambled his way out of skeletal reaching distance.

"Lawrence, you dolt!" Chang stomped to fractured bone. "You're supposed to preserve artifacts, not destroy them."

"You never said we'd find bodies!" Lawrence's pointed a shaking flashlight at the round-eyed skull. "Religious texts, you said. Holy relics."

Chang rolled his eyes. "You can't have religion without people, now can you?"

Jensen pulled Lawrence to his feet. His cheeks were already red from cold, but they flushed more when she brushed away the sand clinging to his back pockets. She smiled. "The bones won't hurt you."

Not the bones, the breeze whispered. Everyone stilled. Shadows darted along the walls.

Jensen cocked her head toward the tunnel. "We should leave."

Chang glared at her. "I give the orders, not you."

The flashlights flickered and died in unison, leaving her holding the only light. She smiled at Chang. "Would you like a candle?"

***

Nylon rustled. Marco poked his head through the tent opening. "Settled in?"

"Almost." Jensen twisted the column of gold hoops lining her ear cartilage while she examined the equipment she'd inherited. She'd turned a wooden crate on its side to get double use out of it. Spare clothes were stacked neatly on top. Reference books stood in alphabetical order inside. Notebooks and pens filled a separate crate. Hammers, picks, and brushes hung in the corner, organized by length. Her predecessor had left them in a messy bundle. Not so messy now. It would have to do.

Marco raised an eyebrow. "It took you no time to build your nest, eh?" He strode in with a large envelope in his hand.

She finger-combed her hair and sprinkled the sand from her fingertips. "I like to be efficient."

"I can tell. We started this expedition three weeks ago, and during that time, Jonas never organized anything." He scratched his chin and looked her over. "Do you happen to have your paperwork on you?"

"Paperwork?" She glanced around the small space. "What paperwork?"

"You know, expedition waiver, medical profile, etcetera." He watched her face and frowned. "Mister Chang said he didn't have anything on file for you. Normally we talk to the helicopter pilots too, but you showed up before any of us woke."

"Ah." She licked her lips. "I couldn't return home without paperwork, could I?"

"The opposite." He handed her the envelope. "Without the waiver, you can't be here. You shouldn't have even gone with us to the cave."

She lifted the flap and pulled out the handful of papers. "What happened to the man I replaced?"

"Jonas?" Marco stared at the books in the crate. "We think he fell. Mister Chang found his broken body on the edge of camp." He glanced at her. "Honestly, I didn't think Mister Chang would replace him so quickly."

She said nothing and leafed through the stack of papers. Nothing in the words said she forfeited her soul. She signed each, and handed them back.

"Good!" He slid the papers back into the envelope and waved her to the tent opening. "I'll show you where everything is in the camp."

She stepped into the thin night air. Stars crowded the dark canvas of cloudless sky. Steam puffed from a community tent, carrying with it the scent of rehydrated mashed potatoes with excessive butter and salted cream gravy. The wind kicked up a flurry of ice chips too dry to be called snow.

Marco pointed to some insulated canisters. "Water. Potassium hydroxide for cleaning. Everyone is expected to pitch in with chores. You can prepare food in the cook tent. We're living on rations until the next helicopter shipment, but Mister Chang always makes sure we have more than enough." He shot her a covert glance. "He does have his good points."

She held up her hands. "Everyone does."

His shoulders relaxed and he motioned to a large stretch of nylon tacked to the mountainside—not quite a tent, but it extended out like one and molded over a frame. He held the flap and zipped it closed after they entered.

Her breath rushed out and she craned her neck to look up. It was so large from this angle. Her chest swelled.

He laughed. "Strange, isn't it? Who would've thought we'd find a giant egg on top of a mountain?"

She ran her hand over the smooth shell. Subtle warmth spread through her fingertips. She pressed her cheek to the surface, a stark contrast to the weather outside.

He caressed the shell. "We still haven't unearthed all of it. I'd guestimate it's over 45 meters in circumference. Beth thinks it's a stone generating a thermal reaction, but I say our jaunt into the cavern proves otherwise." He pointed to a set of shelves built into the egg's support frame and the lamp they had found, sitting in the center. "This thing. This is odd. The round bowl style was used in the Chalcolithic Age, but all the Chalcolithic Age lamps were red clay. This might be one of the first bronze lamps made. When I held it, I got this...feeling—you ever get one of those feelings? That you're in the presence of something ancient?"

She lifted her cheek from the egg and shook her head. "Can't say that I have."

He gave a weak smile. "I guess it's just me."

She motioned to the lamp. "I never got to see it in the cavern. May I have a look now?"

Raised voices reached them from beyond the tent walls. Chang's voice drifted in. "Lawrence! How can you be so stupid? Give me that!"

"S-Sorry," came the hurt reply.

Marco grimaced and licked his lips. He picked up the lamp from the shelf. "I wish he wasn't so hard on everyone."

A loud crack reverberated through the night, and the mountain rumbled a reply. Nylon tent walls shuddered.

Treasures tumbled from wooden shelves and skittered across the floor. Rock creaked once more and settled into deafening silence.

Screams pierced the calm. Marco bolted from the tent. Jensen tried to follow. As she reached the entrance, another form slammed into her, knocking both of them back inside. Lawrence continued to kick and claw, and the rough tread of his boot dug into her thigh and then stomach. She flinched and threw her hands in front of her face. Her palms took the brunt of the damage. He scrambled to the shelves and curled into himself, covering his head and rocking back and forth.

She looked from the tent flap to the trembling boy. With a wince, she rose and hobbled to him. "Lawrence, sweetie, tell me what happened?" She stroked his hair.

"He...he..." He whimpered and dove into her arms, clutching her around the middle. Her ribs groaned. "It's my fault. I shouldn't have spilled."

The tent shuddered around them again. Marco burst in, dragging Beth behind him. Wild brown eyes dropped to stare at Lawrence clinging to Jensen's lap. "Get up. The mountainside is about to avalanche. We need to head to the cave."

Beth yanked free and ran to the corner. Tears spilled from red-rimmed eyes, though the color fled from the rest of her face. Equipment clattered as she grabbed scattered objects.

Marco half-growled, half-screamed. "We don't have time!"

"It's not going to do us any fucking good if we're trapped in a goddamned hole without a way of telling someone where the fuck we are!" She gripped the equipment tighter and glared at him, daring him to argue.

Jensen wrestled free of Lawrence's grip and urged him to his feet. They stepped out into an icy blast and ran for the cave entrance several yards up treacherous mountainside. The rest of the campsite blazed with fire. It stood in a column over a dark puddle of mush and bones. The smokeless flame tilted its bright red-orange head back and stared at her. Hair rose on her neck and arms. She cast a glance at the material surrounding the egg. It wouldn't burn, would it?

The mountain rumbled and chunks of ice tumbled toward the campsite.

"Jensen!" Marco shouted. "Come on!"

She plunged after her companions into the darkness of the cave.

They walked without talking, but the wind and creaking mountain filled in for their lack of conversation. Finally, they reached the cavern deep within and the wind abruptly died. Their flashlights flickered, but stayed on. For now. Sand shifted beneath their boots, sending grains bumping and bumbling to the edges.

Beth dumped their equipment and stumbled to the closest wall. Her body heaved. Undigested matter splattered the stone with the acrid stench of mashed potatoes and stomach acid.

Jensen settled Lawrence next to the bags and looked at the others. "What happened?"

Beth straightened and wiped her mouth. "Not entirely sure. Saw sparks near the water container when Mister Chang was refilling the cook pot. Next thing I know, the thing fucking exploded. Hit the mountain. Mountain broke, hit the potassium hydroxide. Mix that with boiling water and you have a shoddy-ass job of alkaline hydrolysis. Damn stupid way to die."

Lawrence whimpered and rocked back and forth, hands over his ears.

Marco rubbed his temples. "Language, please."

She flung a hand toward the cavern's mouth. "Our boss is a fucking puddle! I think this fucking calls for profanity."

Lawrence stopped his rocking. "Puddle, puddle, puddle. My fault. I shouldn't have spilled. I was making tomato soup—" He cupped a hand over his mouth and heaved, but his hand remained unsoiled when he pulled it away. "He melted. He *melted*. He looked just like the soup. It dripped off him, skin and blood and muscle. Creamy, chunky tomato soup."

Marco compressed his lips and jutted his chin toward Lawrence. "Jensen, do what you can for him. Beth, grab a flashlight and come with me. We need to see if this cave's going to come down on our heads."

The two stomped off; leaving Jensen with the boy's muffled mumbles about soup.

"Plop, plop." Lawrence pretended to drop something. "There went his eyeballs."

She turned to the mess of mismatched equipment and bags. "Will you help me organize this?"

His unfocused eyes lifted. He wiped his nose with his sleeve and nodded.

She picked up a black box with an antenna, red light bulbs, and two metallic knobs. "What do you suppose this is?" She fiddled with the knobs and the top light bulb flicked on. Static crackled from the box.

"H-High powered radio." He sucked in a shuddering breath and took it from her. His deft fingers twisted the second knob, but the static continued without change. He clicked it off, dropped it on the pile, and picked up the closest object to him. "Why'd she grab this?"

The bronze lamp sat in his palms. Whispers shivered through the chamber. Sand slithered and a faint glow emanated from his eyes. The flashlight beam flickered, then died.

Jensen swallowed in the sudden darkness. She patted her pockets. Where were those candles? She found one in her in her side pants pocket, along with the matchbox. She struck a match. The flame flared to life, a miniature version of the one outside. It undulated before her, gathered itself into a ball, and hopped from match head to candlewick without her urging. Her throat tightened, and she dropped the charred matchstick in the sand.

Lawrence stared at the lamp in his hands, turning it back

and forth. "Coming to this mountain was a bad idea. I only did it 'cause Mom said I should. She said it was a chance to impress Mister Chang. She's his secretary. Was anyways." The shadows gathered, pressing in despite the candlelight. Tendrils of darkness slithered up his coat arm, but he never looked down. They picked at his collar and toyed with the ends of his hair. He swatted absently at them.

Jensen clenched her teeth. "Uh, Lawrence..."

"I don't know what Mom will do now. Maybe she can find a better job. Mister Chang paid well, but he wasn't a good boss." The tendrils spread across his shoulders and curled their way down his front.

She scooted closer and held out her hand. "How about you give me the lamp and take this candle instead?"

He sighed. "I wish I was at home right now."

"Lawrence, no!" She lunged forward.

Darkness swallowed him. The lamp hit the sand.

She clenched her fist around the candle. Flame sputtered. She glared at it.

Marco and Beth returned, kicking sand and arguing with each other. His flashlight beam arched across the cavern and landed on her. "We likely won't be crushed by the mountain, but...what? What's wrong? Where's Lawrence?"

She held up a hand and squinted into the light. "Gone."

Beth stomped to the equipment and started yanking items from bags. "Where the hell did he go?"

Jensen swallowed. "Home?"

The two others stared at her. Marco's mouth dropped open. Then he straightened, cupped a hand to his mouth, and shouted, "Lawrence! Get back here!"

No one responded.

"You were supposed to watch him." He shone his flashlight toward the cavern mouth. "Which way did he go? I'll go find him."

She shook her head. "He didn't go any direction. He just disappeared."

Beth raked a hand through her hair. "First Mister Chang,

and now Lawrence. That's a 40% decrease in under an hour. At this rate, we'll all be dead in an hour and a half."

Marco whipped the flashlight in her direction. "The boy isn't dead."

Beth's nostrils flared. "Then there has to be a rational explanation. Just like Mister Chang. The heating unit on the water tank must've fritzed. Had to be something like that. Started sending out terahertz flashes or something. Yeah, that's it. That's probably how the water boiled. And then…" She yanked her glasses from her face and rubbed them furiously with her shirt. "Pressure. Steam? Maybe the steam built up enough pressure to burst the container. Steam could do that, right?" She replaced her glasses and nodded. "Yes, logical. And there's an equally logical reason why Lawrence isn't responding. He's dead. He's dead, somewhere in this cavern, because he couldn't have snuck past us in the tunnel. I just need to find his body."

Marco touched her shoulder. "Calm down. He's not dead."

She lashed out an arm to knock his hand away. "People don't just disappear!"

The three of them stared at each other. Silence hung thick, disturbed only by the slight rasping of breath. Puffs of steam rose from each exhalation.

Jensen cleared her throat. "Did you grab food?"

Beth sneered and lunged at her. Fingers caught Jensen's throat and slammed her head into the ground. "You! This is your fault! Where's Lawrence? What did you do to him?"

The back of Jensen's skull struck over and over. Sand spilled into her ears and eyes. It clogged her mouth and nose.

Marco wrestled Beth off and kept her locked in a choke hold. "Stop it! Strangling her isn't going to get us answers."

"She's the fucking anomaly! She shows up and acts like she owns the whole damn mountain. I'm telling you, she's responsible!"

Jensen rolled over, coughing and shaking her head. She scooted away from the fuming woman. "I didn't *do* anything to Lawrence. He said he wished he was at home. Then he disappeared."

"He wished..." Marco's face paled. He closed his eyes and dropped his hold to bury his face in his palms. "I did that to him."

Beth stumbled forward, but didn't attack again other than shooting daggers from her glare. "What? What did you do to him?" She frowned and studied him. "Did you say something to Lawrence to make him run?"

He dropped his hands. Weariness wove lines across his forehead and around his eyes. "I wished Mister Chang wasn't so hard on people."

"Mister Chang..." Beth covered her mouth with a hand and turned a slight shade of green. "Well, being a puddle certainly isn't structurally *hard*, though he's probably frozen that way by now. But don't be stupid, wishes don't magically come true."

"Like your wish for the flashlights to work? Or Lawrence's wish to go home?" He waved his hand to the cavern. "This must be a sacred place. I could feel it when we entered. Something ancient must live within these shadows."

Beth shook her head. "Not scientifically possible. And if you're not going to look for our lost team member, I will." She spotted the radio on the pile. After snatching it, she dove back into the cavern's mouth. "Lawrence!"

Jensen pulled out another candle and lit it. She sank it in the sand until it stood on its own.

Marco turned his attention to their surroundings and wandered slowly, gaze trained on the image-laden walls instead of the sand. His flashlight beam halted on one segment. "Come look at this." He pointed, outlining the figure of a bird resting atop an egg. "This is probably the egg we found outside. And this looks like writing. Arabic?"

She rose and left the equipment. "Kufic, one of the earliest forms of Arabic calligraphy."

Marco shook his finger at the wall. "I know this story. Aladdin. In the original story, a magician convinced Aladdin to fetch the lamp, because he could only receive it from the hand of another." He moved the light along the wall. "Here, the magician's brother tricked Aladdin into asking for a roc's egg to hang in the dome."

She studied the depicted scene, gaze lingering on a figure of fire. She read the text beneath it to herself.

"Wretch!" he cried, "is it not enough that I have done everything for you, but you must command me to bring my master and hang him up in the midst of this dome?"

Marco rubbed his face. "The French translators used 'genie' as it was the closest they could come to jinnī." He looked at her. "You probably know more about the jinn than I do."

She glanced back to the lamp lying on the ground, and the candle seated next to it. "They're described as smokeless flame."

He looked at the lamp, strode to it, and picked it up.

The candle flame leapt next to it, a tiny being on arms and legs. It didn't stay small for long. Scorching flame spread until it licked the ceiling. The equipment melted. Plastic popped and snapped in a malicious cackle. Noxious fumes billowed out from the inferno.

Marco started coughing. "Jensen!"

She ran to him and together they flew for the entrance. Heat blasted them from behind. A whoosh of air flung them forward. His foot struck something and he fell with a startled cry. He rolled onto his side, gripping his leg to his chest. "My ankle! You get out of here. Find Beth and—"

Jensen reached down. "Give me the lamp."

His face tensed. "Why?" An explosion thrust another heat wave barreling at them.

Things had to be difficult. She stooped and grabbed him beneath his arm. With a small grunt, she hoisted him to his good foot, braced him, and ran, ignoring his limp. Cold air struck her face. She spotted a silhouette standing in a pool of white light, waving wildly toward the sky. A helicopter hovered above their heads, blades slicing flurries of snow from the air. Someone dressed in black rappelled down a nylon rope and landed next to Beth. "We can only transport two of you," he shouted over the mixed noise of machinery and wind. "We'll have to come back for the others."

Jensen carried Marco to the light. "Take him first, he's injured."

Beth clutched a discharged warning flare in one hand and cast a hesitant glance at her. "You can go."

Jensen shook her head. "Go on. I'm used to this weather."

A look of vast relief spread across Beth's face and her shoulders slumped. "Thank you."

The black-clad man nodded and set to tying the big man into a harness. The rope jerked tight and the lamp slipped from Marco's grip. He gasped and reached for it, but it hit the snow at Beth's feet.

She picked it up and frowned. "Is that a picture of a bird?"

Marco stared at her, and then looked at Jensen. He glanced from the cavern down to the egg. His Adam's apple bobbed when he swallowed. His eyes went wide, and they shot back to Jensen.

She smiled.

His mouth opened, but the wind stole his words and the rope jerked him into the sky.

They sent down the line again.

Beth reached for it with one hand. Her other hand stretched back and laid the lamp in Jensen's upturned palms.

The man in black motioned to the others in the helicopter and leaned close to Jensen. "Hang tight. We'll be back." Then the line pulled him up.

The mechanical beast dove into the night, pushing its light in front of it.

Jensen pulled the matches from her pocket. She struck one and flung it toward the campsite. It whipped through the air, carried by the wind, but the flame never extinguished. It struck the lingering hydrogen gas from the potassium hydroxide and water reaction. The campsite exploded. Snow crashed down the mountainside, wiping out the last of the tents.

The flame stalked from the cavern, its fiery maw parted with a smile of pointed teeth. It bowed. "Where have you been, master?"

She glared at it. "That detestable magician traps me on another world, and the first thing you ask me is where have *I* been?" She shook the lamp. "What have you been doing in my absence? I return to find these humans invading my home and this..." She pointed at the cavern. "What is this doing on my mountain?"

The flame flinched. "The magician sent a human, Aladdin, for the lamp. Aladdin refused to hand it over, and then discovered me bound within. That wretch commanded me to build him a palace. I moved it here after he died to keep it close to the child." A flame hand waved toward the undamaged egg.

She pursed her lips. "I see. Humans have an annoying way of holding on to what doesn't belong to them." She worked the tight knot in her boot laces with her fingernails. Finally, the leather unraveled, and the calf-high suede slumped to her ankles. She lifted and wiggled her feet until the boots fell off. She unbuttoned the thick moleskin trousers and slid them off her hips. The socks came off with them and landed in a pile on top of her boots.

The flame undulated beside her. "Supernatural creatures have a hard time with the hand-off rule. At least someone eventually gave you the lamp."

"I would've had to follow them, if not." She stripped off her shirt and tossed it aside with the rest of her clothes. Free. Finally. "Do me a favor and get rid of the palace."

The flame nodded and vanished, along with the cave.

Sharp claws of feral wind raked at her, trying to snatch her up and carry her out over open ground. She growled, flung out her arms, and dared the elements to take her. She had faced them before. They hadn't been able to keep their hold on her. Her hair unraveled and whipped about her. Wings sprang from the markings Chang had called tattoos. Feathers sprouted across her flesh. Her talons dug into the cliff face of Mount Qaf.

She lunged into open air.

About Loni

Loni Townsend:
Wife. Mother. Writer. Ninja. Squirrel.

By day, she writes code. By predawn darkness, she writes fantasies. All other times, she writes in her head.

People call her peculiar with a twisted sense of fashion, but don't let those understatements fool you. Her behavior is perfectly normal for a squirrel disguised as a human. That's part of being a ninja—blending in.

She makes her home in Idaho with her sadistically clever—yet often thwarted—husband, two frighteningly brilliant children, and three sneaky little shibas.

Find her on her blog (http://lonitownsend.com), and pick up her epic fantasy, Thanmir War, or her fantasy humor novella, *This World Bites*, on Amazon.

THE GOLDEN PEN

Marlie Harris

"You need to sign here, please." The delivery man shifted from one foot to the other as I took the electronic gadget from his hand and signed the screen. His brown suit was wrinkled. I wondered if he even knew what an iron was. *Whatever happened to caring about yourself?*

I should talk. I'm in my pajamas and it's 10 o'clock. I handed him the thing back and took the package from him.

"Do you know who it's from?"

"We don't track who sends what, ma'am. Unless they pay more." His voice carried the bored expression far more eloquently than his bearded face. I glanced at his name tag.

"Thanks anyway, Steve." *You asshole*, I thought.

He looked up from his gadget, "Have a nice day, Mrs. Stanley." His grin didn't cover the sarcasm very well.

"You too, Stevie boy." I closed the door, wishing I could slam it and looked at the small brown package in my hand.

To:
Laura Stanley
15311 North Cormorant Place
Eagle, ID 83616
To be opened by addressee only.

No return address, but the postmark was from Ridge Falls, Idaho.

My old home town. Crazy Dazy Ridge Falls.

THE SEVEN

Who the hell would send me something? No one knows my address.
***

Ridge Falls, Idaho. I was born there. I would like to say I had a great childhood there. But that would be a lie. Ridge Falls wasn't a good town. Sure, all the residents were supposed to be normal. But that was on the outside. Inside, it was dark, dank, and filled with evil or something akin to it. Growing up there made you one of the special ones. My mother used to say, "If you are born here, you are marked."

I had no idea what that meant. I looked over my body so many times. I'd asked lovers to check me, doctors. No one found a mark anywhere. I wasn't marked at all.

But people had a way of dying in strange ways in Ridge Falls. Those were rumors, although no one actually talked about it. It was sort of unspoken.

I remember one time, though. When mom and some of her friends were in the kitchen at the table drinking tea. The weekly gathering was supposed to be a way for the women to sample different teas and play cards. Truthfully, it was to catch up on all the latest gossip. I had come inside from playing in the fields, thirsty. I walked quietly from the front door toward the entryway to the kitchen. Mom's voice rose above the chatter, "You remember when Sherry was killed?"

The complete silence that followed her statement made me stop in my tracks. *Who was Sherry? When did she die?* My mind, as a young artist, flowed with ideas.

"Jenny, we don't talk about that." Grace was my mom's best friend. "Her death was ruled an accident."

"Oh come on, Gracie. You know better. Your dad was the sheriff then. Remember? All her bones were broken and her brain was sucked out. You came to school the next day and told us. Remember?" Mom's voice carried that high pitched note. The one that came with knowing the truth and being unheard.

"Shut up, Jenny. I never said anything like that. I would remember and I don't. Now get me some more chamomile tea, will you? I think that's my new favorite."

"You haven't even touched your first cup."

"I don't care, Jenny, dammit. Get me some more."

There was another silence, filled with unspoken tension.

"Fine, Grace. I'll get you a new cup. That one is probably cold anyway." I heard my mother's chair slide back and her nursing shoes squeak as she crossed the kitchen. "What hand are we on now, girls?"

"Threes, I think." Mrs. Genner flicked her lighter open, then I heard her expel the smoky air from her lungs in a cough. "Get back here and win us this hand, will ya, Jenny?"

The chatter resumed as if nothing had happened. I went into the kitchen, got my drink, and ran back outside. My mother's voice followed me, "Laura, do not let those boys rough-house with you!"

"Yes, Mom," I called over my shoulder, same old answer to the same old statement. The day was getting old. I didn't want to miss any more of it. But I didn't forget about Sherry. I just filed her away until later. Because I was determined to find out what had happened to her. If my mom was that freaked out, I wanted to find out why.

My best friend Jackie always said an evil had been let loose when they built the dam. Her grandfather was one of the ones who argued against it.

So when I went to her house the next Saturday, I knew she would be happy with the research I was going to suggest. She believed the rumors, so would be the perfect person to help me.

We were outside when I decided to ask her.

"So Jackie, you want to find out something cool with me?"

Jackie was swinging a bat we'd found in her garage against the post far out in the field behind her house. The metal bat made a pinging noise every time she hit the post.

"What cool thing?"

Ping.

"I heard that someone was killed a while ago. Her name was Sherry. Her brains were sucked out."

"How do you know?"

Ping.

"My mom and her friends were talking and I overheard them. My mom said Sherry was killed. Her friend Gracie's dad was the sheriff then, but Grace acted funny when mom brought it up. I think there's something weird about it."

Ping. The sound bounced inside my head like a runaway tennis ball.

"What kind of weird? Do you think she was murdered?"

"Maybe, but not in a normal knife or gun way. I think there was something strange about the way she died. Mom wouldn't say her brains were sucked out and all her bones were broken unless she sort of believed it."

Ping.

"Jackie, please stop hitting the post. It's making my teeth ache. Would you just listen to me?"

Jackie stopped and leaned on the bat. "Okay, so you usually make fun of me when I tell you about what my grandpa said. Why do you believe this story now?"

I sighed as I felt my blood pounding behind my eyes. "Because my mother doesn't believe hokey shit. So if she said it, then something must true about it. At least I think so. Are you interested or not?"

PING.

After one final swing, Jackie settled the bat on her shoulder. "Sure, let's go see if there is something at the library."

Thankfully, the library was on her side of town. The walk was warm, but not too hot. We were happy to be inside in the cool by the time we arrived.

"I'll see if Mrs. James will let us use the Microfiche machine without standing over us." Jackie was always good at making people believe her when she promised something. Of course, she always did what she said, so adults never had any reason to doubt her. I heard her tell Mrs. James that she was helping me do research on a family tree project, and would make sure I didn't mess anything up.

Mrs. James graciously told her to go ahead and take as long as she wanted. Part of me was jealous, but the other part wanted to know if we could find anything. I smoothed down my t-shirt and nodded to Mrs. James as I walked with Jackie toward the back. I bit my lip so I wouldn't smile. The coppery taste kept me straight-faced.

The library's microfiche room was located behind the main receiving area. The librarian stood or sat behind her desk or the counter checking out books. The room was bordered by shelves that held hundreds of trays of microfiche containing newspapers and magazines. Jackie rummaged and came up with a box from the Ridge Falls Gazette.

We sat down at the first viewer, the white light diffused, so not quite blinding. She slipped the first slide into the slot and leaned forward to look at it. The newspaper headline across the top of the screen read:

Ridge Falls Gazette
LOCAL GIRL FOUND DEAD

Ridge Falls Reservoir claims another victim. Sherry Blakney's body was found dead in South Park Hole. The medical examiner has no comment on the cause of death at this time. The Blakney family requests that flowers be sent to Ridge Falls Funeral Home...

There was more, but the screen went black. Even blacker than the normal dark grey when there was no electricity.

"Hey, Jackie, I wasn't finished." I put my hand on her shoulder.

Jackie jumped, "I didn't turn it off, Laura. It wasn't me."

I noticed at the upper edge of the screen, where fluid started to bulge and roll down. Tenebrous sable glistened as it strung downward. The rivulets migrated toward the center, collecting into a mass of jet black. The blob seemed to absorb light, while the strands glistened.

Jackie gasped and slid back. I was fascinated. I couldn't help myself.

"What is it, I wonder?" My voice sounded as if it came from somewhere down a long, tin tunnel.

"I don't know and I don't care, this is crazy. Let's get out of here!"

The pulsating thing grew out, as if reaching for something. My head seemed to pulsate as I stretched my hand out to meet it.

Jackie slapped my wrist. "What the hell do you think you're doing, Laura? Let's get the fuck out of here."

Jackie's cussing woke me. "You never cuss, Jackie." I felt sluggish, confused, like I was in a sand trap up to my neck. I could barely move.

Jackie grabbed my arm, digging her fingers into my bicep. She drug me out as I still reached for the blob which also reached out for me.

I stumbled after her, struggling to keep my feet. "Hey, Jackie! You don't have to pinch. Jesus, I'm coming."

She didn't let go until we were out the door and standing in the hall outside the microfiche room. Then she whirled, inches from my face.

"What. The. Hell. Did you think you were doing? Do you know what that was?" Her breath was hot and sweet. I blinked, trying to get my bearings. The pounding in my head was so distracting. I felt an urge to go back in.

"I don't know what you're talking about, Jackie. We were looking for information about that girl that died. The next thing I know, you're dragging me outta there and screaming in my face."

Her green eyes squinted at me, trying to determine if I was lying.

God, I hope she buys it! I gotta play stupid.

Jackie sucked on the inside of her lip, not moving away. I kept my eyes steady. The pulsating beat in my head seemed to ease. Fear set in. *What was that?*

Finally, she stepped back, sighing.

"Fine. You obviously don't remember what just happened. You got hit with Ridge Falls' Sickness. That's what grandpa calls it. I've never seen it before, but I've listened to enough stories from him to know what happened."

She rubbed the area of my arm that was red from her grip. "I'm sorry, Laura. You scared the shit out of me."

I shook my head, "It's okay, Jackie. My mom said I was marked a long time ago, I guess you just found the mark." I smiled, hoping she would get the joke. My stomach was beginning to unknot itself. I concentrated on relaxing.

She looked at me sternly. "It's not funny, Laura. You could die. Or worse, you know."

"Okay, I'm sorry. I didn't mean to make light of what your grandpa told you. What happened?"

She shivered and rubbed her arms, "This black ooze came out of the screen and started to reach for you, then you started to reach back. I pulled you out before you touched it."

I shrugged, "I honestly don't remember."

Oh yes, I do remember. It was delicious. That feeling of darkness consummation. But I was also afraid of it? What sort of blackness could do that? I craved it.

Jackie slapped my shoulder, "It's good you don't. You wouldn't want to know what happens to people who have touched it. At least, that's what grandpa says."

Yes, actually. Yes, I do want to know.

But I wouldn't find out until I was much older.

***

I walked to the desk, sat, and pulled the dragon letter opener out of the coffee cup I used as a pencil holder. Someone was being environmentally conscious. The box was wrapped in brown paper. I slipped the opener under the edge and sliced it open. The wrapping fell away to reveal a simple white, rectangular box. No writing, no filigree, nothing special about it at all.

My curiosity was definitely piqued. I opened it and looked inside.

"Wow," I breathed, "that's some gift."

A golden feather fountain pen sat inside a lush purple velvet bed. The detail was astounding. I ran my fingertip along the stem and down to the quill. I brushed the vane. It was made of metal and it was warm. January in Idaho was cold, very cold. This box had been in the back of a delivery van.

It's not supposed to be warm, is it? I ran my hand up the vane again. *Is that a tarnished spot?*

I rubbed the spot with my thumb. It didn't come off.

Must be part of the feather.

I picked it up. *It's heavier than I thought. The edge of the vane looks sharp.*

I ran my finger along it.

Ouch!

My blood slowly rolled down one of the feathered grooves.

Stupid pen.

I set it back into its plush bed.

"I do not have time for this shit." I got up went to get a Band-Aid. "I need to finish this fucking story."

The small slice throbbed, but no more blood flowed. I covered the cut.

Back to work, dammit.

My frustration was palpable. I couldn't breathe and swallowing was so damned hard. I suffered from a classic case of writer's block.

Will this work now? I don't know for how long. But I do know it's making me angry. I can't keep doing this. Trying to write. There is nothing coming out of my brain.

My mind feels like it's going to explode out of my ears. Why can't I think of anything?

My eyes ventured down to the white box sitting next to my keyboard.

I wonder who would send me such an expensive pen.

Is it really gold?

I opened the box again, stared at the contents.

It's so beautiful. I wonder where it was made?

I picked it up, turning it in my hands, running my thumb along the quill once more.

"A long time ago and far away." I looked up. Standing in front of my desk was a man who could have been mistaken for homeless. His patchwork clothing choices made me think, at first, that someone had broken into my house. I glanced around, everything seemed in place. My office door was closed. I stood up quickly, holding the pen out in front of me like a sword.

"Who the hell are you and how did you get in here?" I figured I was a lot stronger than this scrawny guy.

I can take him.

The gentleman shuffled his feet in place. He grabbed his beard and pulled down. It obviously didn't move very well.

"Don't make me ask again. Who are you?"

"I am Gentry. Who are you, and why did you summon me?"

"Summon you? What do you mean, summon you?" This was getting weird, but my artist mind put things together. *Is this what I think it is?*

"You summoned me from the pen, you idiot. Now tell me who you are and what wishes I can grant you."

I looked down at the golden pen in my hand. "How did I summon you? I thought I was supposed to rub you or clean you or something."

Gentry pulled his beard again. I swear I thought I saw something move inside. "That's an old wives tale. You bled on my vessel. That's the calling."

He stood up straighter and intoned, "When the blood of the desperate is shed on your prison, you will come to grant two wishes."

I noticed his eyes glinted redly. Through the bushy eyebrows, I couldn't be sure though.

"I thought it was three."

"Are you even listening to me? Two wishes, blood on my vessel. That's it. No more. Now, what do you want?"

"Is this real? Maybe I'm daydreaming. I mean, I don't

really know if it is, right?" I turned away from my desk to walk toward the door.

In an instant, I was face to face with the hairy, unkempt Gentry. His eyes truly glowed red. "Don't turn away from me like that."

I felt an iron grip on both my arms as I was raised up, turned, and pushed against the wall next to me.

"Ooof!" My breath burst out of me as my back slammed against the wall. I realized I was a foot or so above the floor, my feet dangling.

"Do not turn away from Gentry Beleth… Ever!"

A spiked pain began in my head, above my right eye. Smoke rose from his hair, his face contorted and his pupils disappeared. His nose tilted pig-like. The old man was gone. In his place stood a demon-like creature.

"I will take your eye for your insolence." The thing raised its pointed finger and moved it toward my eye. The fingernail was sharp and gently curved, dirty.

Oh shit, I'm dead!

The clawed finger stopped two inches away. I stared at it. The glistening black nail wiggled in front of my eye. The demon pulled back, then jabbed again. I couldn't help but blink. His hand stopped two inches away again.

I thought his scream would pierce my eardrums. The demon dropped me and I crumpled to the floor.

"I can't harm you, you measly little sack of meat." He became Gentry again and his shoulders slumped in defeat. "I cannot injure you. You are marked."

I cleared my throat and sat up. "What? I'm marked? What the hell?"

It felt like splinters imbedded themselves in my throat.

He looked at the ceiling, ruminating, his eyes dim pink. "You bled on the pen, so you've been chosen, but even before that, you were marked. The one who calls me can't be harmed. But you've been marked before, by another, so I couldn't anyway."

I rubbed the back of my neck. "What about others?

Friends or family of mine. Can you harm them?"

Gentry shook his head and tugged on his beard. "No, no one can see me or interact with me except those who are called."

I stood up slowly. "So, if you can't hurt me, then how were you able to slam me against the wall. I felt like I was gonna die."

"It means with an intent to kill or injure you. I didn't say I couldn't touch you at all. And if you look, you'll see there is no harm to you. Even though it feels like it." His eyes glowed red again and I shivered.

"So... um, what should I wish for?"

"The rest of the fairy tale is true, you can't wish for more wishes, you can't wish someone dead."

"I hadn't heard that one, about wishing someone dead."

He shrugged. "Yeah, well, that one was because we demons are happy to collect souls, and killing for others is a pretty easy way to do that."

I shivered again. *What the hell? I don't remember this part of the fairytale.*

"Okay, so, I need to find out more about how the wishes work before I make mine."

Gentry looked at me so long, I thought he would throw me against the wall again. "You sound exactly like Poe. Do you know that? He wanted to know more too."

I shakily brushed past him, walked to my chair, and sat. "As in Edgar Allan? That Poe?"

"Who else would I be talking about?" His smile revealed ragged teeth. *They look sharp.*

My skin crawled. "No one, I guess. So who else have you come to?" I had to figure out what to do with this.

"I help artists. Didn't you figure that out yet?" He walked around my desk and slid into the chair directly in front of me. "So, what are your wishes?"

"First, who are you? I've never heard of Gentry Beleth. Are you a new demon?"

Smoke began to rise from his mess of tangled hair. "You

little… I was a king."

He stood again and struck a pose, his resonate baritone voice boomed, "Beleth is a great king and a terrible, riding on a pale horsse, before whome go trumpets, and all kind of melodious musick. When he is called up by an exorcist, he appeareth rough and furious, to deceive him."

He slumped down in the chair, once more, sighing. "Johann always knew how to make me feel special. I miss the old fart."

My mouth closed with a snap. "Wow, that's pretty, wow; I don't know what to say. It's nice to meet you, sir."

He looked at me with red eyed cunning, "Don't patronize me, youngster. I know you're stalling. Just make your wishes already."

"But you didn't tell me who else you've helped, or granted wishes to. Poe died. Did you kill him?"

The red flared. "I told you, I cannot kill a human. Poe killed himself."

"Fine, but who else did you help? Are any still alive? Did they live a long time?"

The demon started ticking off on his fingers, "Socrates, died from ingesting poison, not my fault. Michelangelo, died at 88, not my fault. Dusty Springfield died of breast cancer, also not my fault."

"Great, so everyone you've helped is dead. That makes me feel really good." I rubbed the tightness in the back of my neck, again.

Beleth grinned. "You all die. You are human."

Good point.

I swallowed the dust bunny in my throat, "Okay, I guess, I don't get much time to think this over, huh?"

The homeless troll demon shook his head, smiling.

I thought quickly. *What can I wish for? More money? What?*

Then I had it. It came to me as I looked at my computer. I remembered the frustration I felt earlier. I didn't ever have enough time to write anymore. *What if I had plenty of time to write?*

As my mind imagined what it would be like to sit and have the words flow from my boiling brain through my shoulders and down to my fingers. I saw myself typing furiously, bent over the keyboard, laughing delightedly. *What if I never lacked for ideas?*

I looked past Beleth, through the window. The peach tree was drooping with fruit. Around the tree were late blooming flowers. I never could remember their names. The landlady took care of them. She told me one time as I walked up the driveway what they were. I'd acted pleasingly smooth, but I didn't bother remembering. Flower names never interested me. Their colors were a different story. I loved the bursts of colors from flowers. How each seemed to have their own personality. Pretty purple, posh pink, garish green, blushing burgundy, rotten red. They grew throughout the summer and burst into bloom at the end of the season, their petals only glowing for a few weeks. Time was short for them, too.

But, what if it doesn't have to be? What if I had more time and more ideas? I could write for the rest of my life. Just write stories. Peace came over me as I thought of this nirvana.

I took a deep breath and looked up at Gentry. "I wish I had more time. I wish to have writing ideas for the rest of my life. That's what I want to wish for. I wish I had more time to write and I wish I had all the ideas to write for the rest of my life."

Gentry Beleth smiled sweetly, "Are you sure, my little friend? Is that what you really want?"

My mind churned to find the problem. I couldn't see one. "Yes, that's what I really want."

"Good. Now package up the pen and I'll give you an address to put on it. Then you will have your wishes." The red eyed scruffy beast was smiling too much.

What could go wrong? It's everything I have ever wanted.

I placed the golden pen back into its plush, purple box, closed the lid, wrapped it and grabbed a normal pen.

Gentry told me the name and address to write. I didn't recognize it, but that wasn't my worry. I would have what I always wanted. More time to write and more ideas than I could ever need. I couldn't help smiling at the idea of the next schmuck who would prick their finger on the pen's feathered side. *I hope they are as smart as I am. Even if they aren't, I'll still be writing.*

My hand shook as I wrote the address on the outside. *Good luck, whoever you are.*

To:
Terry Snyder
249 Franklin Road
Lincoln, NE 68505
To be opened by addressee only.

"Okay, I'm ready." I sat at the computer, hands poised over the keys.

"Yes, my friend and little meat sack, you are ready." He laughed. The words started to flow into my brain immediately. I could finish this story. It would be outstanding. My brain filled with the light of a million ideas. I didn't notice the pain at first. I was engulfed in the bliss of my mind's eye. Then it hit me harder, racing up my left side. I choked, trying to speak, but nothing came out. My sight misted and grew white, then black. The pain was beyond anything I had experienced. More than fire, more than lightning, it was so hard to breathe.

What's happening to me? What the hell?

I tried to raise my hands. Nothing. The left side of my body was lit up with an ivory crystalline fire, the pain unbearable. I tried to scream. Nothing.

My body leaned forward, I couldn't stop it. My face hit the keyboard as I bounced off the desk. I felt my lip crunch against the space bar. The taste of blood streaked through my mouth. I rolled to the floor on my back. The iron boulder of realization slammed into my brain.

I am paralyzed.

I thought it would never end, but finally, the pain began to fade to a dull ache. My eyes cleared and I saw Beleth standing over me, smiling.

"You humans are so predictable. Did you know Poe asked for the same thing? I don't have to kill you, you little bags of flesh kill yourselves. There is your wish, little one. You have plenty of time to write and you will have amazing ideas." He pulled his beard gleefully. "But you will never be able to write a single word."

This isn't what Aladdin's Lamp does! What the fuck is this?

"Ah, so you thought you had the lamp of Aladdin, eh? No, you do not possess the lamp. The lamp is not the only talisman bearing wishes." His evil chuckle buried itself in my chest. For a moment, it twisted there bringing sharp pain, then it relented, just when I thought I would die. "No, artist, you will not follow Poe to the darkness yet. And you won't find a way to kill yourself. I will make sure you are healthy, you filthy slug. I have learned over the years, I won't suffer for my mistake again. You will live until you are meant to die."

His laughter followed him into the plain brown-wrapped box. I screamed in my head.

***

Now I am stuck in this bed. The doctors say it was a stroke. They said they'd never seen one so pervasive in someone in their thirties. My brother came by that afternoon and found me. If he hadn't, I would have died of starvation right in my office. I know Beleth sent him over. That fucker.

They feed me and I eat. I tried to stop, but my body won't respond. It nourishes itself. It feels like a sand trap. Only I can't move my head either.

They think I want to live.

My brother and his family come by to visit me once a month. The rest of the time I stare at the ceiling while nurses, doctors, and caregivers come and go.

Gentry Beleth was right, I have lots of ideas and I have lots of time.

The television screen just went black. I can see the black tar mass gathering in the middle. I can't move to reach for it this time. But I don't think it will be hard for it to reach me. I know what it is now. I've had plenty of time to understand what it means to be marked. I don't want it to take me. Paralyzed with the liquid black madness inside me.

I can't run.

I can't scream.

I can't even widen my eyes.

I blink slowly.

It's coming closer. I hear the slithering on the linoleum.

The sheets at the foot of the bed rustle.

Kill me, please?

About Marlie

Marlie Harris spent her youth reading Anne Rice, Stephen King, Dean Koontz and then later graduated to Neil Gaimen, Clive Barker, and H.P. Lovecraft. She is a member of the Horror Writers Association of America and Idaho Writers Guild.

The Ridge Falls Series Book 1: *Into the Darkness* is Marlie's first publication. She is currently putting the finishing touches of her debut novel, "Leather" a book set in Ridge Falls and tentatively ready for publication in April 2015. Her passion is to write horror and thriller stories.

Marlie enjoys the outdoors including camping and fishing, but her biggest obsessions are the color green and collecting dragons and her nirvana is a green dragon.

Websites: www.ridgefallsseries.com & www.marlieharris.com
Facebook: http://www.facebook.com/marlie.harris1
Twitter: @mharrisauthor
Instagram: @mharrisauthor

A LAUDER WAY

Rochelle Cunningham

The smell of chocolate chip cookies baking in the oven filled the house. Grace laid down her copy of Diana Gabaldon's *Outlander*. She loved reading in the sunroom of her 1920's historically registered home. The forty-five-year-old romance novelist routinely sat on a sage green, suede loveseat covered in variegated chenille throws and soft, crushed velvet pillows. The entire room was encased with old, sectioned glass windows which allowed natural light in, and provided a view of the golden foothills surrounding her home in the Boise valley. Grace stood, and instantly felt the sensation of the warm hands of her long-deceased Great-Grandma Lauder on her shoulders. The old woman gently guided her through each doorway of the old house; a house she herself once owned.

Grace silenced the stove timer and retrieved the goodies from the oven. Her sixteen-year-old niece would arrive any minute. With fall coming to an end, they still hadn't spent as much time together as they agreed to last Christmas; vowing to set aside one Sunday a month for each other. Morgan was beginning her own busy, independent life. Time slipped away, as it often did, so Grace treasured the moments she had with her niece. She heard the screen door slap and the jingle of keys hitting a table from the other room.

"Hi Auntie!" Her niece's youthful voice filled the old house.

"In the kitchen, baby."

Morgan gave her aunt a big hug, a kiss on the cheek, and grabbed a warm chocolate chip cookie from the platter. "Isn't this one of great grandma's plates?" she asked.

"It was one of her mother's, your Great-Great Grandma Lauder."

"Do you remember her?" asked Morgan.

"I remember visits with her when I was a child. Birthdays. Picking blackberries. The back yard used to be filled with them," Grace told her.

"Your back yard?"

"Yes. The whole back half acre used to be filled with vicious, thorny vines." Grace smiled, remembering her childhood. "We learned to maneuver around in the briar patches with an old coffee can tied around our waist. She fastened the cans with long strips she'd cut from her old dresses, and that's how we gathered berries. I can still taste those fat, juicy, Lauder berries. Nothing like them anymore."

"What happened to them?"

"Aunt Clarabelle cleared the patches out years ago when she owned the place." Grace lowered the heat on a gurgling teapot.

"I like your lilacs better." Morgan reached for another cookie. "Didn't Grandma Lauder write a lot, like you?"

"She kept journals. Years ago I read some I found in an old trunk around here. Grandpa Lauder had his PhD in anthropology, and they traveled quite a bit." Grace thought a lot about her great-grandma. Sometimes, it was impossible to escape her. "What shall we do today, dearest?"

"I got an idea," Morgan said, brushing cookie crumbs from her palms and swiveling her barstool at the breakfast nook to face her aunt. "I thought about this on the way over." Twice a week, Morgan took the bus in from Nampa High to attend morning college courses on the Boise State campus. She was a determined young woman, and Grace admired her spirit. "You're probably going to think I'm a nut."

THE ANCIENT

"I like your nutty ideas. What is it?"

"Remember when I was little and we used to play tea party? The whole ride over I couldn't stop thinking about those parties. Every time I tried to read, the idea would pop back into my head. I want to have one today."

"I love it. But can we make it a grown-up tea party? Out on the back patio? With a hot cup of tea?" Grace suggested. *And milk.* Grace had a sudden craving for milk in her tea.

"Of course," her niece giggled. It was a perfect day for play; a crisp, September morning promising high seventies and lots of sunshine, and plenty of time to encourage their inner-children. They had the whole day before her sister, Ginger, was expected to pick her daughter up for dinner. The three women took time to stay close, enjoying weekend bike rides, hikes in the foothills, candle burning ceremonies, concerts, and now that Morgan was getting older, an occasional glass of wine as they discussed the life plans of their young protégé.

"Earl Grey, Green Tea?" Morgan asked.

"Perfect," Grace confirmed. "And I'd like mine with a little milk, please," she added.

Morgan opened and closed the cupboard doors. "I don't see anything to put the milk in," she reported. "Hey! What about that cute little Aladdin's lamp on your mantle?"

"Make sure you wash it out. Lord knows what's been in it."

Morgan returned from the living room, passing through the kitchen entrance. "Where did you get this, Auntie?"

"It was left here in the house. I don't know if it's ever been used for anything. It belonged to Grandma Lauder, along with that platter, the lamp, and a few of her doilies. They're all I ended up with."

"And the house."

"Yes, I was blessed to have been next in line for that. I am sure she appreciates us using her things today." *If not, I'll hear about it later.* "She took that lamp with her all over the world when she traveled. I remember Mom telling me that."

"Where did she and Grandpa Lauder travel?" Morgan asked, scouring inside the brass belly of the lamp, rinsing it, and then handing it to her aunt to dry.

"Oh, gosh, all over. It's been so long since I've read her entries, I don't recall exactly. I do believe she picked up the lamp somewhere in India, though." Grace wiped the old, brass relic down with a cotton dish towel.

The two ladies shuffled around the whitewashed kitchen setting up for their tea party. They placed small Asian tea cups, saucers, spoons, and honey on an oblong tray. The gold and blue ceramic was inlaid with several dainty sunflowers. The ancient lamp was filled with cold milk and placed in the center. The two women exited through the back kitchen door onto the porch.

Morgan filled her aunt in on her life: school, boys, rugby, art, and photography. She was all over the board with her interests, something that drove her mother crazy, but Grace encouraged. *Ah, she's just where she should be at sixteen*, Grace always thought when Ginger argued with her daughter about another change of heart or new passion.

Morgan finished her first cup of unsweetened tea with a splash of milk. "I would love to travel," she said, closing her eyes and welcoming the sun to warm her smiling face. "Grandma Lauder sounded like a pretty adventurous lady."

"It's in your veins, too, you know," Grace said, knowing of her niece's desire to attend college anywhere but Idaho.

"I'd like to see her journals. Can we go through them some time? I would love to see life through her eyes."

"I don't have the vaguest idea where I saw them last," Grace said, reaching for the napkins as they nearly blew off the table.

Morgan sat up to look at the rose bushes lining her aunt's weathered picket fence. They didn't move. The breeze had vanished as quickly as it came. "Where did that come from?"

Her aunt shrugged. But she knew full well what *that* was.

Don't put off until tomorrow— Grace heard her grandmother whisper on the breeze.

"Well." Morgan slapped both hands down on the arms of the old pine frame chair, "this tea is going straight through me. Excuse me, will you?" Her smile seemed to linger a while there in the back yard, until Grace was disturbed by Morgan's scream.

Grace's heart nearly stopped when she entered the kitchen. The moment she walked through the doorway, her world literally changed.

Stopping dead in her tracks, looking at where her cupboards used to be, she saw twisted jungle vines that draped and hung everywhere. She couldn't believe her eyes. Grace felt a set of fingers, gently lace through her own. The feel of soft, delicate skin adorned with a coolness of silver rings on nearly every finger, assured her it was Morgan.

"Auntie?"

"Yes?"

"What the hell was in that tea?"

The two women stood listening to the scurrying sounds of monkeys in the treetops above and the chatter of toucans in the branches nearby. Off in the distance a very large cat let out a mournful growl. The two women stood holding hands in what used to be Grace's kitchen.

"I'm officially uncomfortable," Morgan offered calmly. She was much more composed than Grace imagined she would be.

"It's alright." Grace wasn't sure if she was trying to convince the sixteen-year-old at her side, or herself. While she wrapped her mind around what was happening to them, and attempted to remain calm, she was relieved that nothing had lunged at or swooped down for them so far.

"Is this for real?" Morgan asked.

"You're seeing what I'm seeing. Right?" Grace responded with a question of her own.

"Yeah."

"Then, I'm guessing, it's for real."

Grace took a step forward. Morgan squeezed her fingers tightly around her aunt's, and followed. They walked along a dense, spongy forest floor where Grace's black and white checkered tile used to be, mindful of their steps to avoid the vinyl skinned creatures on the path. Nearing the living room doorway, they saw a wall of mist escaping from a waterfall several stories high. From beyond the mist, came a voice, an invite from beyond. It rose on a bold, tropical wind beckoning them to cross over.

"Well?" Grace looked at her niece. Morgan grinned.

"I'm in, if you are," she challenged her aunt.

With their free hands, both of them reached as if to part the fog like a set of drapes. Piercing sunlight exposed them. Adjusting to the light, they surveyed miles of sunbathed grasslands with various mammals roaming about. Grace nodded toward the grazing hippos, elephants, and guinea pigs, as jackals darted among the absent-minded herds. Morgan pointed out the giraffes with their heads peering above the leafy trees as though they were eating from the top of a green cotton candy spindle. The leopards kept a safe distance, draping themselves among the more naked tree branches as though they had not a care in the world.

"Africa?" Morgan offered.

"Possibly."

Inching toward the hallway, and away from the grasslands, a desert stretched out so far it appeared endless. A caravan of camels carrying natives swathed in loose, vibrant fabrics passed in front of them. Grace and Morgan jumped back to avoid being trampled. After the last stinky camel passed, the girls noticed the sun beating down on their heads and felt their shoulders beginning to cook with the intense heat.

"Here," Grace guided her niece, placing both of their backs against the wall, "we'll scoot down the hallway."

"To what?"

"I have no idea, Morgan."

A dusty wind picked up. They put their heads down and migrated toward Grace's room. Entering the grand master bedroom, the two women dropped, as if the floor had vanished, falling several feet into a large body of water.

Gasping for air as they surfaced, they reached for one another and then swam to shore, crawling onto the crystal white shoreline.

"*What* is going on?" Morgan said, out of breath.

"We've fallen through some kind of wormhole."

"No, I believe we fell into a lagoon!" Then Morgan let out a belly laugh so unexpected and delightful Grace took a moment to giggle with her niece on the warm, white sand. "I have to say, this is, by far, one of the best ways to spend an afternoon, Auntie." She wiped the wet strands of hair off of her face. "But how do we get outta here?"

Grace had no idea. "It's always best to try and return to where you started." She rolled over to check out her surroundings. *What a beautiful island*, she thought, while gathering her sense of direction. "My bedroom window leads to the patio. Let's try to get back out there."

"And, where might your window be?"

Looking around at the thick, island grasses shaded beneath a forest of palms, Grace stood up to brush the sand from her nearly dry skin. "Follow me," she instructed, heading toward the foliage. For several minutes they listened to the waves gently slap against the shoreline as they pushed their way through the tropical greenery.

"Are you sure it's in here?"

"I'm not sure of anything. But I'm guessing, if this is my bedroom closet over here," Grace thumped around, feeling her way, "then the window will be right through—"

"Auntie Grace?"

"It is! I feel it, right here," and with a slight grunt, she popped her window open and the smell of the familiar Idaho back yard merged with the island breeze. Grace located the bottom sill of her window and blindly raised the glass enough for the two of them to climb out. Lopping themselves out onto the cobblestones lining the back patio, they realized they had come full circle, back to where they left their tea party. The two highly perplexed, half-soaked travelers slumped back down into their chairs.

"Auntie," Morgan broke the long silence, "I know that *'things'* happen to you. I've heard that you feel things, hear things, I get it. No judgment," Morgan looked over at the kitchen door and took a deep breath, "but, holy crap! You never said anything about this. What gives?"

Grace rarely talked to anyone about her supernatural experiences. Her family was the last to believe her, and she was having a hard time believing this herself. Mainly because nothing like this had ever happened to her before. All she could do was shake her head. Morgan was right. *Holy crap!*

"Let's do it again!" Morgan nearly squealed.

Grace looked toward the kitchen. "I don't know how we did it the first time." None of what happened seemed to frighten Morgan, and Grace was impressed.

"Let's figure it out." Morgan reached out her hand to her aunt. Grace folded her fingers inside of her niece's and they walked toward the screen door. As they stepped into the kitchen, they were filled with disappointment. It was Grace's old shabby chic whitewashed kitchen, with everything neatly in place.

"Awhhh, how do we get it back?" Morgan pouted.

"I don't know, honey."

The two went back for more tea.

"Come on Great-Great Grandma. Show me some more!" Morgan poured herself a plain cup of tea.

"Do you really want to know what happens around here?" Grace held her cup with both hands, deciding to confide in her niece. "Great Grandma Lauder is with me all the time. Guiding me. Placing things in my sight. Moving shit around. She is always trying to communicate."

"I knew it! Seriously?"

"But I don't know how she's doing this. It's nothing like I've ever experienced." She noticed her niece scrutinizing her every word. "Never, Morgan. Maybe we're making the connection stronger by talking about her."

"It's the house."

"It's not the house. I've been here for years, it's not the house. It's her, somehow, she's trying to cross over."

"It's a cosmic brrridge," Morgan rolled her 'r's and spoke with flowing hand motions in the air. "She's trying to brrridge the generation gap!" She leaned back in her chair, pleased with her theatrical pun. "I don't know either. But who cares?"

Morgan's confidence overwhelmed Grace. It was as though she already knew the answers, and knowing was much less important than doing. Grace envied her, wishing she had that kind of blind faith. "Maybe we're over thinking it. Maybe she just wants to take us on a tour of her favorite places? Did she have a favorite place?"

"When your mom, and Aunt Gabbie and I, were just little girls, I remember sitting around on her back porch like we are now – but surrounded by gardenia bushes. Many of them grew so tall that they actually turned into trees with blossoms the size of dinner plates. This back yard was a magical place. I remember her making fresh raspberry iced tea and we would sit out here, shaded by those trees. I'm sure she probably told us stories of all the places she had been. I don't remember, but I think your mother asked her the same thing one time."

"What did she say?"

"She looked at us girls, and she said her favorite place was right here next to us."

"Where were the gardenias?"

"Where all the lilacs are now – surrounding the property line. They froze out years ago and no one ever replaced them. They're tough to grow in cold climates. But she made them. Her kids always said she could grow anything."

"That's where grandma gets it." It was true. Grace's mother had the greenest thumb of anyone she'd known.

"We've got to go back," Morgan insisted.

"I'd rather have another cup of tea," Grace looked into Morgan's green, cat-like eyes and was ashamed she hadn't seen it before. Morgan said nothing, but her sparkling eyes returned an understanding smile as she reached for the honey bear. She had psychic connections, too. Grace was certain. "No honey this time," Grace said. "Just a little milk, please."

Morgan returned the golden plastic bear to the tray and picked up the Aladdin's lamp instead. "Mom thinks you hear voices."

"A lot of people think a lot of things," she said and noticed the disappointed look on her niece's face. She had dismissed her again, a habit she would have to break. Grace took a sip of her tea, and cleared her throat to start over. "I don't hear voices. I feel things. Sometimes it's like the flutter of a butterfly's wings, little things off in the distance, a blur or vibration. Other times I feel the presence of those who have died; they guide me, protect me, sometimes they calm me. And once in a while, I'll hear sounds like a whisper - something audible from somewhere else. But it's not a voice."

"I think it's cool." They drank their tea and stared at the kitchen door.

"I think you're cool," Grace said.

They both sat their cups down and looked away from the backdoor screen at the same time.

"It's time, Auntie. No more stalling. We gotta try this again!"

Crossing through the threshold the two stepped onto what used to be the long runner-rug leading from the back door into the center of the kitchen. It was now a dirt path leading into the jungle. The damp smell of the rainforest tickled Grace's nose and she giggled.

"What is so funny?"

"You wanted to be back in the jungle – here we are!"

"Are you serious?" Morgan asked her aunt. "What jungle? You can see it?"

Grace was confused, but Morgan wasn't. A look came over her face and she lit up like a kid on Christmas morning. She pulled her aunt out of the kitchen.

"It's the lamp! I drank my tea plain, while you had milk in yours." Before Grace could object, Morgan's certainty rushed her back to the table for another cup of tea, using great-great-grandma's lamp to add some magic. Grace was impressed at her niece's understanding of the supernatural.

"Great Grandma Lauder? Are you in here?" Grace called out from inside her jungle kitchen. She and Morgan heard no reply. Instead, from behind the bushes where her stove used to be, something rattled and the foliage parted. A young boy wearing a tribal loincloth peeked out from his hiding spot. He held a long spear and wore a bright white smile that gleamed against the darkness of his skin. He turned and disappeared as quickly as he had come.

The two stood spellbound, looking up at the treetops where a super-highway of howler and spider monkeys converged with neon hummingbirds darting in and around clusters of glorious macaws and swollen beaked toucans. Hues of colorful reptiles scurried along the branches high above. Yellow, green, and purple anacondas negotiated with brightly striped or speckled iguanas as to the appropriate crossings. Meanwhile neighboring micro teiid lizards, coral snakes, and speckled poison arrow frogs determined their path of least resistance.

Morgan pointed at a mother rhinoceros bathing her little ones in a large, murky Amazon pond at the base of a waterfall. The slow growl of a jaguar in the distance finally melted their trance and the two of them made their way down the path leading toward the living room.

Stepping into the room, the beautiful plains of Africa stretched out further than their eyes could see. Grace nodded toward her sun porch and the villages of thatched roofs and colorful dots bobbing on the horizon that had to be baskets belonging to native women as they balanced them atop their heads. Black and white striped zebras and cheetah herds grazed quietly in her living room on honey colored grasses. Noticing a family of spiky porcupines waddling around, as giant vultures and eagles soared high above, the girls began to hear drums and yelp-like singing coming from painted faces that danced around a distant campfire.

"Oh, let's get closer!" Morgan insisted.

After a moment's hesitation, Grace's adventurous nature led the two of them onward. They quickly discovered they were merely guests in this world with a restrictive pass. It was much like walking around inside a giant snow globe, with only an invite to be part of the landscape.

From the cover of the tall grasses, Grace and Morgan laid down to watch a lion and her cubs play under a lone tree. A large winged crane and a couple of buzzards glided, and swooped overhead. The two visitors took time to laugh and roll in the grass, taking in the world around them, until an ominous swirl of clouds formed in the distance and the clumsy drumbeat of thunder began. They scurried to the edge of the living room, in the direction of the hallway, until they found themselves on the edge of the Sahara Desert.

Another caravan moseyed past, or it could have been the same one from earlier. Who could tell? The camel's adornments jingled as they walked by, bearing trunks and passengers. Herders yelled foreign-tongued commands at their sheep and long haired goats.

"How beautiful," Morgan commented to her aunt, and pointed to the women atop the camels. They were dressed in vibrant sheer fabrics and matching head dresses that waived behind them, the jeweled fringes glinting in the sunshine. Grace stood, mesmerized by the sea of tangerine oranges, ruby reds, and flickering golds, until someone in the caravan spoke to her, breaking the spell.

"You look just like her," a man riding a two-hump camel said, flashing a friendly gap-toothed grin.

"I look like who?" Grace asked.

"The doctor's wife. You both do." He smiled and rode on.

Grace and Morgan exchanged looks, and giggled. By the time they looked back, the man was barely visible in the distance. They felt the hot desert sand between their toes and knew they couldn't stay long.

"Back to the jungle?" Morgan asked.

"Time for a swim!" Grace corrected.

"To the island it is!"

Better prepared this time, the two wormhole travelers jumped through the bedroom doorway into the teal green water surrounded by a pale, iridescent beach. They splashed down and laughed their way back to shore.

Lying flat on her back, looking up at the clear blue sky, Grace realized the importance of sharing in other peoples' dreams.

"I wish I knew what island she visited," Morgan wondered, echoing her aunt's thoughts.

"Jamaica? Or maybe one of the little islands off the Bahamas."

"This feels pretty secluded. Maybe Grandpa wanted to get her *alone*," Morgan said, and they both giggled.

"How is she doing this?" Grace pondered out loud.

"I don't know. But what an amazing gift, right?"

"Promise me something?" Grace rolled over to face her niece, thinking light years ahead. "Promise you'll remember this." Morgan looked back at her as though she'd lost her mind. How could anyone forget something like this? "We'll remember it when we're on the other side. Maybe we can both give this adventure to someone - like Grandma is giving it to us," Grace told her niece.

"The secret is finding someone who will let you give them such a gift," Morgan said, completely comprehending the reality of the situation. "But that's why I love you, Auntie. I always knew you could connect to the other side. But never, in my wildest dreams, did I think it could be like this."

"Neither did I, my love. Neither did I," Grace responded.

Then Morgan surprised Grace yet again. "Do you know I've been waiting a long time for you, Auntie Grace?"

"What? Waiting for me?"

"Yes. For a very, long time."

"How long have you known, Morgan?" Grace supposed that hanging out together on a deserted beach in her bedroom, created from her dead grandmother's memories, was as good a place as any to have this talk.

"Longer than you." Morgan stared up at the blue heavens. Somehow she knew all about Grace's supernatural connection, long before she did. "Remember when Mom was so sick, you guys thought she was gonna die?"

What? She was only a few months old.

Morgan continued. "She was delirious. Grandma and Aunt Gabbie went in the other room while you stayed by her bed and held her hand."

"You were a baby in your crib. Every time we tried to take you out of the room, you let out the most blood curdling howls."

"I remember. I didn't want to leave her side." Morgan breathed in the sweet island air. "But I also remember what you prayed for."

Grace turned in Morgan's direction. She had never told a soul what she had prayed for that night at her sister's bedside. There was no way she could know.

"You told the Almighty, the Forces Unknown, Maker of All Things, that if he took her, he would have to make room for you, too. You refused to live without your sister. You insisted he show you he was listening. Then you levitated off the ground where you had been on your knees, weeping, desperate, and angry. You said you would become the instrument he had been asking you to become, a request you frequently denied. You traded your sister, and my mother's life, for an open-ended supernatural contract."

Grace couldn't move. Her heart was so full of love and admiration for her niece, she thought she might burst at the seams right there on their multi-generational island.

"I know I'm only sixteen, but I have never seen love like that, Auntie Grace. And I've been waiting a long time for you."

Tears flooded Grace's eyes. "You can read people's

minds?"

"No. It's more like sound waves and only if someone is in a deep state of concentration. So I guess you can say that I read meditations, or prayers. And I saw yours."

Grace let out a heavy sigh. "Looks like we have a lot to talk about."

"Indeed," Morgan answered as her tummy growled. The two women realized they hadn't eaten.

"Can you think of a better place to have a picnic, than the African plains?" Morgan asked, changing the subject and forcing some fun back into their day.

"No ma'am. But how about lunch on the porch, and a cookie on a blanket in Africa?"

"Agreed." The psychic travelers plundered their way back through the island greenery, located the window, and staggered around to the kitchen to make some lunch.

"Best frickin' tea party ever!" Morgan held up a teacup to clink with her aunt after finishing a tuna sandwich and a fruit bowl.

"Best frickin' tea party in the history of tea parties!" Grace agreed, sharing the toast with her niece.

The day was nearly over when they emptied the last of the milk from the lamp.

"One more time?" Morgan requested, and Grace filled the lamp for one last adventure before Ginger arrived to pick up Morgan for the evening.

But the kitchen remained the kitchen. The magic was over.

"Oh, Auntie Grace. We had one lamp's full of free passes to some of her memories. Do you think we'll ever get another invite?"

"I don't know. I suppose we'll have to schedule more tea parties. After today, my sweet – I think anything is possible."

"Grandma Lauder had a heck of a life," Morgan said.

"She must have carried that lamp around with her everywhere. We were pouring just a few of her memories into our tea. Imagine what else she has to show us." Grace said, and Morgan smiled at such a romantic notion. As the two women sat at the table, exhausted from globe trekking, they heard a familiar voice from the front of the house.

"Anybody alive in here?" Ginger hollered. Grace and Morgan laughed at the complexity of such a question. Grace's baby sister, and Morgan's mother, joined them on the back porch for a brief visit. Ginger was always in such a rush, but Grace didn't have any objection today. Especially since she and Morgan were having a heck of a time making up an excuse for why they were so worn out.

Ginger shot both of them an exasperated look. "Alright then, you two. Let's go, Morgan." Hugs were exchanged by the sisters, then kisses and hand holding between Grace and Morgan. Ginger's lemon yellow VW backed out of Grace's driveway. Before the car reached the street, Grace turned back to the sound of her niece's voice.

"Auntie!" she hollered, perched out of the passenger window, "do you smell that?"

Grace lifted her nose to the evening air. She nodded and smiled back at her beautiful niece, who was waving to her like a rodeo queen with a secret.

Gardenias!

About Rochelle

Rochelle Cunningham, author of the children's book series: "Waiting on Daddy's Hug", and inspirational guide, "The Writer's Handbook" due out in February, is currently developing "Envy", a short novella; one in another collection of supernatural thrillers by *The Seven*.

A WISH TO GIVE

Sherry Briscoe

Garibaldi winds were stronger than usual, blowing the vendor tents over onto the nearby railroad tracks. It was the worst Garibaldi Days Abigail had seen in over thirty years. Rain, wind, and unseasonable cold for the end of July. This was not good for their tourist trade. The little fishing village didn't have much, as it offered no beaches, condos, or large attractions, but was just a blip on the map between other popular towns on the Oregon coast.

Abigail owned Pirate's Plunder, a spacious antique store on the main street of town. She stood and watched as the wind threatened to blow all the vendors out into the marina. She shivered. *Thank God I'm indoors.*

A young couple dressed in spandex sportswear, walked in the store, Abigail figured mostly to get out of the wind. But she stood up anyway to greet them. The small rhinestones set in her cat eye-rimmed glasses glittered when the sunlight through the window hit them. Her gray frizzy hair had a mind of its own, and seemed to shift direction depending on which way you looked at it.

"Pretty windy out there, isn't it? Looking for anything specific?" Abigail asked.

The man ignored her and walked into the book and record section. The woman smiled politely. "Do you have any bottled water? That wind has blown dust in my face and mouth. It's just terrible." She made a nasty facial expression.

Abigail shook her head. "No, I sell antique bottles, but none with water in them. You could try the convenience store across the street at the gas station."

The woman looked back out the window. "Oh yeah. Say, you wouldn't happen to have a brass lamp, you know, like Aladdin's?"

Abigail sighed. "Sorry, no lamps either. But you're welcome to browse the items I do have." She tilted her head at the young woman, smiled and sat back down. She picked up the worn paperback romance novel and resumed reading it.

The woman nodded as the couple left.ABigail looked up over the top of her glasses at them. "Yuppies," she muttered, and flipped the page.

As the weekend drew to a close, the tourists left, the vendors packed up their unsold items and gear, and the wind continued to blow as the town returned to its quiet self. August was just around the corner, hopefully with warmer, less windy days ahead. Cars passed Pirate's Plunder, but rarely stopped. Abigail turned the closed sign around, locked the front door, turned off the lights, and made her way to the back of the store and up the narrow stairs to her apartment above.

Abigail's small living space was quaint. The walls were covered with an eclectic pattern of photos, artwork, and plates she had acquired from the store. Every time she found something she liked, she brought it up and found a place to squeeze it in. Nothing on her walls matched, in the same way nothing she wore matched. Abigail was a free spirit who loved patterns and colors and thought of herself as a walking rainbow. She smiled.

The next morning, her dear friend Lizzy and her very fat cat, Buddha, arrived just as Abigail was opening the store. Lizzy put Buddha down and the large black and white feline waddled through the store to investigate and search for possible rodents. Lizzy was a young widow and a talented artist, although these days she created more pottery than she painted, citing something about a cursed ancient Chinese paint brush. Abigail couldn't remember exactly. No matter, she loved company. She lived upstairs and worked downstairs by herself, and led a very solitary life.

Lizzy placed her elbows on the glass counter and propped her chin in her palms. "Abbie, you need to get out of this place. Take a vacation. Now that Garibaldi Days are over, it'll be like a ghost town for a while."

Abigail huffed. "Where would I go, and what would I do? My whole life is here."

"Exactly, you need a break dear. I don't know, go up to Seattle, eat some fresh fish on the pier, shop in the market place."

"But what if someone came to shop? I can't just leave the store."

Lizzy looked around the large rooms of antiques, books, records and clothes. The one thing missing was customers. "I'm having my house painted in a couple of days, and the smell of fresh paint gives me terrible headaches. Buddha and I could stay here while they do that, and we'll watch the store while you get some fresh air, out of town." She smiled with an 'I dare you not to go' look in her eye.

Abigail shrugged her shoulders and looked around. "I suppose I could go to Pike's Place Market, haven't been there in years. It is fun. But I'm just so comfortable here, I hate the thought of leaving."

Lizzy gave her an understanding look. "I know. I felt the same way right after Doug died. I didn't want to leave my house at all, for months. But Abigail St. George you need to get out of here for at least a little while."

"It's scary out there. It's safe here."

Lizzy nodded. "I know. I had that same feeling too. But you can venture out. Everything will still be here when you return."

Abigail stood up and threw her arms in the air. "Okay, okay. I'll go to Seattle. You promise to be good to all my customers?" She smiled.

They both looked around the empty store.

Tuesday came and Lizzy entered Pirate's Plunder carrying an overnight bag. She carried Buddha in and sat him behind the counter.

Abigail came down the stairs, a small suitcase bouncing behind her. "Lizzy, thank you so much for this. I am starting to actually look forward to this trip."

Lizzy smiled and brushed her straight black hair behind her left ear. "Don't worry, I'm happy to do it. It gives us both a little diversity from our daily routine."

"Well, I'm all packed. Is there anything from Seattle you'd like? I'll bring you back a souvenir."

Lizzy shook her head. "Not that I can think of. And you don't need to bring me back a thing."

Abigail hugged her. "Oh honey, I'm happy to. You guys just make yourselves at home. I'll call you and let you know when I'm heading back down." Abigail handed her a key ring with a dragon on it that held several dangling keys.

"No worries. Which route are you taking?" Lizzy asked.

"I'm going to drive up 101, take the scenic route through Astoria. It's about four hours either way, and 101 is much prettier."

Lizzy smiled. "I couldn't agree more. Just drive safe and let me know if you need me to do anything special while you're gone."

Abigail hugged Lizzy then headed to the back of the store. "I'm going out the back door. I'll call you when I get to Seattle."

Lizzy sat in the comfortable chair behind the glass counter and pulled a current issue of *Pottery Making Illustrated* out of her tote bag.

As soon as Abigail got out of Garibaldi, the clouds lifted and she saw the blue skies over the Pacific Ocean. She hummed a favorite tune as she drove up the highway, her windows rolled down feeling the rush of the ocean air circulate through her car and through her hair. She loved driving.

THE ANCIENT

Seattle was busy when she reached city center. Abigail drove to Pike's Place Market, her favorite place. She watched the men throw fish, then smelled the beautiful fresh cut flowers, and passed through the various stands of home grown and handmade products. There was something about this city that made her come alive. She closed her eyes and smiled as she expanded her lungs and her chest, pulling in a deep breath.

"Ah, Seattle," Abigail said. "How I've missed you dear friend." She giggled to herself, bought some fresh roasted almonds and walked along the shops past the market.

It was warm and sunny, unusual for Seattle, and the sounds of the harbor were like music to Abigail's ears. She strolled along the sidewalk and a sparkle in the window of a small shop caught her eye. She turned to look and saw a dainty brass lamp on a shelf. She raised an eyebrow. *Aladdin's lamp*, she thought. *Just like the yuppie in my shop wanted. She should have come here.*

Abigail started to walk past, but turned to look at the tiny lamp again, and decided to go in and check it out.

The store was small inside, nothing like her place in Garibaldi. It was dimly lit with dark wood paneling walls and floors. The brass lamp in the window caught the sunlight and lit the whole room. At least that's how it felt to her. She reached over and picked it up, and a tingle traveled down her left leg. *How odd*, she thought. She turned the lamp around to inspect it. It had a delicate pattern in the brass, and a chain that connected the lid to the handle. *How smart.* It wasn't much, only fifteen dollars. She probably couldn't resell it for a profit, but it might look nice on a shelf in her apartment. She bought the lamp with cash.

Abigail sat in an open air dining area at the Waterfront Park and ate fish and chips. It just didn't get any better than this. She licked her fingers and smacked her lips. It felt surprisingly good to be out of the store for a while.

After she finished eating, Abigail walked back up the street to the Seattle Marriott Waterfront, where she had booked an ocean view room. On the way she picked up a bottle of Pinot Noir to end the evening with.

Abigail sat on her bed with all the pillows propped up behind her back, a new Dean Koontz novel she'd bought on her walk, and a glass of red wine on the night stand. She had opened the windows to hear and smell the scent of heaven just outside. She glanced over at the small brass lamp that now sat on the small table in the corner of the room.

"I know what it feels like," Abigail said to the lamp. "If there was a genie in there, how cramped and confined it would be, pinned in, unable to escape. Hmm." She thought for a moment. "Much the way I've felt lately at my shop. Safe and comfortable inside, not sure of the unknown that lurks beyond." She looked back at the lamp. "You must feel the same way."

Abigail finished off two glasses of wine before she recorked the bottle, turned the light off and slumped down under the covers to fall asleep.

Rain came in the night, as it often does in Seattle. It beat on the glass so hard it woke Abigail up. She had forgotten to shut one of the windows and the floor was getting wet. She pulled herself out of bed and slid the window closed. As she turned, she noticed the little brass lamp was gone. She searched her thoughts, but was sure it was on the table when she went to sleep.

Abigail turned on the light beside her bed and looked all around for it. The lamp wasn't on the table, or the floor. It hadn't rolled under the bed. She held her lower back and grunted as she got to her feet. Getting old was not the easiest on her body. She looked in her suitcase, thinking maybe she put it away without remembering, but it wasn't there either.

Sitting on the side of the bed, Abigail picked up the bottle of wine and looked at it. "How much did I drink? And what did I do with that lamp?" She looked around, rubbed her tired eyes, turned the light off and slid back under the covers. Just as she was falling back to sleep, she heard a soft voice that seemed to come from everywhere in the room, yet nowhere in particular. She turned to look at the window. Lightning lit up the sky outside and cast an eerie shadow across her room.

"Is someone there?" Abigail timidly called out, hoping of course, that no one would answer.

"You have thirty hours to grant three wishes."

"What do you mean? Grant wishes? I can't grant wishes! And to who?" Abigail sat up a little, holding the blanket up to her face, exposing only her searching eyes. But she still saw no one. "Hello?"

"You have thirty hours to grant three wishes. If you do not fulfill this bargain, you will be consumed by the dark."

"Bargain? What bargain, wait just a minute there, I never made any bar..." Abigail stopped mid-sentence. *Where in the hell was that damn brass lamp?*

"Hello? Can you at least tell me who I'm supposed to grant wishes to?" Abigail trembled a little under her blankets. But no answer came. Thunder billowed outside her window so loud it shook the glass and Abigail jumped. Then she scooted down into the soft folds of the bed and pulled the blanket over her head.

"Me grant wishes?" Abigail muttered. "I don't have any power. Did the lamp give me some?" She thought for a moment, sat up quickly and looked around the room again. "Did the lamp give me power to grant wishes?" she called out, but no answer came. The thunder rumbled out over Puget Sound moving away from her window, away from the shore.

Assuming she had drank too much wine, and so was having one hell of a dream, Abigail drifted back to sleep. She didn't hear the voice whispering in her ear like musical notes on a page. "You only have three wishes to give, use them wisely to live."

The morning seagulls screeched outside Abigail's hotel window. She sat up on the edge of her bed, rubbed her eyes, and looked out to discover a pale blue sky that made her smile. She waddled over to the counter, stretching her back, and started the small coffee pot. She yawned and looked around the room taking inventory. Half-drunk bottle of wine, couple of books on the table, her suitcase, shoes, handbag, but no brass lamp. Surely she didn't dream she bought the thing? And yet, it clearly was not here.

Abigail soaked in a hot bubbly bath that relaxed her and loosened up her muscles. She held her right hand up to wash her arm when she noticed a strange mark, just above her wrist. It looked like a tattoo of some sort. She watched as the black line spread until it completed a number 3, and then stopped. The mark burned. She tried to wash it off, but it wouldn't budge. It was as permanent as any tattoo done in a professional parlor. This mark felt wrong and evil, and she would have cut off her hand if she thought she could. She slid down under the layer of bubbles, searching the room for someone who might be watching her. She was almost afraid to get out of the tub, but stood up and grabbed the towel quickly off the rack, wrapping it around herself. She stood staring at the number 3 that now covered a space about three inches square just above her right wrist. She felt a touch of panic run through her veins.

What magic is this? Abigail wondered. She dried herself off, quickly pulled her clothes on and poured the coffee. The caffeine felt good running through her system, the jolt of energy, life, and just plain yummy. She loved coffee. She took in a deep breath and looked at her wrist again. It would be hard not to look at it now.

Abigail pulled her shoulder bag across her chest, adjusting it securely for the morning walk. She brushed her hair, applied her new Hot Kiss Red lipstick, and headed out the door. She walked the few blocks up to the market place and smiled, as best she could, at the morning breeze, the smell of the marina, and the sounds of the sea. She felt sorry for all the millions of people that lived so far inland they didn't get to experience the coast every day the way she did. It was her life blood, the salt water, the hypnotizing waves that never ceased to make their way in and out. It was beautiful.

Walking along, Abigail passed by the store where she bought the lamp. She quickly ducked in the doorway and approached the old man behind the counter, his face covered in white whiskers. He dusted empty shelves.

"Excuse me, can you help me?" Abigail asked, her heart pounding at the thought of how ridiculous she was going to sound.

His hazy blue eyes looked over at her and he nodded. "Do my best."

All of a sudden Abigail's throat was so dry she could barely form a word. "I-I bought a small brass lamp in here yesterday. It was over there, in the window." She turned and pointed to the place where the lamp had been. She shook as she held her right hand up to the counter, for the old man to see her tattooed number 3.

"Tsk, tsk," he said as he shook his head.

Abigail quickly withdrew her hand and covered it up with the other one. She felt embarrassed. She didn't know what to say or do.

The old man softened his tone. "Listen, you're not the first. It's a cruel trick he plays, turning things around like that. Best I can say is go find someone willing to tell you a wish they want."

Abigail nearly started to cry, her chin quivered. "But then what do I do? I don't know how..." She sniffled and rubbed her nose.

"You'll know when the time comes. Listen, and open up your heart. You have the power now. Do what you have to do." He wiped the counter down with a damp towel and walked into the shadows in the back of the dim room.

Abigail rubbed at her wrist wishing she could rub the mark off. But the harder she rubbed, the more it burned. She put her head down and headed out the door, scared and alone. She never felt this way in her store in Garibaldi. Even when she was the only one in the building, it never felt lonely. The ornaments and art she had collected over the years had become her friends in a way. But now, here on the chilly streets of Seattle, she felt isolated.

People began to fill the shops, restaurants, and walkways. Pike's Place Market was full, congested, and loud. Abigail pulled her sleeves down to cover the dark mark on her arm, but with each passing hour, the number burned deeper into her skin. It filled her with a sense of urgency. She needed to desperately find someone who was willing to confide in her a wish they truly wanted. The more she searched, the more she felt she would never find anyone. People turned away from her as she approached.

Abigail finally left the crowds and walked down to the edge of the sound at Waterfront Park. She sat on the large deck and watched the tide advance, retreat, and advance again. She loved its determination. She inhaled long deep breaths, not just to savor the salty air of the Pacific, but to take in the resolve of the waves.

A family walked in her direction, whistling to a dog, although there was none in sight. The parents whistled while the young boy, probably five or six years old, called out for his lost pet.

The little boy walked up to Abigail. "Have you seen a spotted dog? His name is Buddy, and we can't find him."

Abigail felt his pain as if it was her own. Her heart raced with fear for the pet that could be in danger, or even worse. She put her hand on the little boy's. "Do you wish for me to help you find your dog?" The way she spoke frightened the boy. He took a step back.

"I just want my dog to be back home safe with me." His little brown eyes searched her face for some kind of answer. Just then the dog came running from behind the crowd and nearly knocked the boy down with his exuberant licks and tail wagging.

Abigail's heart sank. *So close*, she thought. She watched a couple holding hands and thought she would try them. She walked over, but as soon as she neared them, they got up and walked away. She panicked more every minute. What

THE ANCIENT

was she to do?

Abigail walked into a small art gallery near the pier, and looked at a beautiful custom designed ring. The clerk behind the counter walked up. "Can I help you?"

Abigail smiled. I'm just browsing right now. But I wonder if there's anything I could do for you?"

The clerk looked at Abigail, confused. "What do you mean?"

"If there was a wish you could have, what would that be?" Abigail asked.

The clerk rolled her eyes. "Look lady, I doubt you're my fairy godmother, so if you're not going to buy something, I have to get back to work."

Abigail's heart hit rock bottom. She walked out of the store and across the street to a small kitchen shop. She was going to have to do some creative thinking if she was going to make it through this ordeal alive. Her arm burned with increasing pain. She walked around the store and when another customer came in, she discreetly walked up to the lady customer.

"Can I help you?" Abigail asked the new customer, hoping the real store clerk wouldn't hear her.

The woman frowned at her. "No, I think I'm fine." She walked away.

Abigail went back outside, found a bench to sit on and cried. She couldn't do it. She sobbed. "Doesn't anyone have something they really want?"

At that moment a young woman walked past Abigail. She stopped and looked down at her. "We all want something, what do you want?"

Abigail looked up at the cute blond through teary eyes. "I just want to grant you a wish. One wish, tell me one thing you want." She sniffled and wiped her nose with a tissue from her pocket.

The young woman looked at Abigail for a moment, deciding what to do. She smiled. "I want to get the job I just interviewed for. Can you grant me that wish?"

Shoving the tissue back in her pocket, Abigail stood up and smiled at the woman. "Oddly enough, I think I can. With all the power I have, I say the job is yours."

They looked at each other for a minute without words. Neither one really knew what to say next. The young woman's cell phone rang and she answered.

"Yes, this is Anita. I got the job? Thank you! Yes, of course." She glanced over at Abigail as she walked to the corner of the block.

Abigail waited a bit, took a deep breath and held it as she pulled up her sleeve. Sure enough, the 3 was fading, and in its place a 2 appeared. She let the air out of her lungs and laughed. That was easy enough, she thought, and walked up to the marketplace to find another wish to grant.

Abigail walked up to a middle-aged woman dressed in black looking at flowers. "What wish do you have today?"

The woman looked at Abigail as she put the flowers down. "What are you talking about?"

Abigail sensed hesitation in her voice. "I mean, aren't these flowers beautiful?"

The woman looked at her suspiciously, turned and walked away.

Abigail tried again. She walked up to a young couple walking hand in hand, admiring all the booths in the marketplace. "Beautiful day, isn't it?"

The young man looked at Abigail and frowned. "Piss off, lady." He nudged his girlfriend to turn and go another direction.

The afternoon continued with one rejection after another. Abigail couldn't even strike up a decent conversation with anyone. *I've got it*, she thought, *I'll go to a bar. Everyone likes to talk in a bar.* She headed down the street and found a small pub, walked in and sat at the counter.

The bartender was a jolly enough looking man in his mid-forties, head shaved completely bald with a salt and pepper goatee that was in badly need of a trim. He placed a cardboard coaster in front of Abigail. "What'll it be?" he

THE ANCIENT

asked.

Abigail smiled as she looked around the small, dimly lit place and looked into his emerald green eyes. "Draft beer will be fine. Something dark."

The bartender turned and poured a glass of dark ale and placed it in front of her. "That'll be four-fifty."

Abigail opened her pocketbook and placed a five dollar bill on the counter. The bartender scooped it up and replaced it with two quarters. She took a drink of the beer and decided it was a pretty good brew.

Abigail looked at the man next to her, hunched over on his bar stool, wearing shabby clothes, sporting a two-day old beard stubble. She wondered if she gave him a brush if he would at least run it through his hair, but then she realized if he did, she would probably have to throw the brush away.

"Hi, my name's Abigail." She stared at the man for a moment, but he never looked up from his beer, although he did grunt something unintelligible.

"If you could wish for anything, what would you wish for?" She waited for the man to answer.

The man looked over at Abigail and frowned. "I'd wish for you to shut up and leave me alone."

Abigail's eyes grew big in horror. *Oh dear*, she thought, *this is not going well at all.* Unable to control what she was doing, she got off her stool, backed up all the way to the door and left the bar.

She tried to open her mouth, but her lips were stuck together. She reached for the door handle to go back inside, but a force field kept her from even touching it. Her fingers could not get within five inches of the knob. She gulped and ran down the street and into an alley. She walked up to a small park area and sat down on a bench. It took nearly an hour before she could open her mouth again. She looked at her wrist. The 2 had disappeared and was now replaced with a large black number 1.

"I must be more careful," Abigail said to the two little squirrels scouring the ground in front of her. She watched them for a moment. "I don't suppose you have a wish? Some more nuts for winter, maybe?" The squirrels ran up the tree and were quickly out of sight. She dropped her gaze to the grass in front of her. "No, I suppose not," she muttered.

The number 1 was burning so deep in her wrist it was beginning to ooze blood around the edges, and the pain seared up her entire arm. Abigail whimpered. She held her wrist close to her chest and stumbled back toward her hotel. She was at a complete loss at what to do next. She realized now how evil this was, and worried she would not be able to win this deathly game. Her chin and lips quivered at the idea of her approaching end. A tear slipped down her cheek, she quickly brushed it aside.

Abigail walked down to her favorite spot at the edge of the water and watched the waves once more. *I wonder if there's any fish in there that have a wish?* She half chuckled to herself. If her life was to be over soon because of the black magic in some godforsaken brass lamp, she would at least spend her last moments in the place she loved best, at the ocean's edge. The seagulls flew above her and squawked in the air. The salty breeze gave her a sense of peace and joy, she closed her eyes and smiled.

She glanced down at the blood beginning to ooze even more from her wrist. Abigail realized it would look like she took her own life. *What a strange way to end my story*, she thought. She was sure even rushing to the hospital would not do any good. They would not be able to stop the pain, or prevent the death that would soon take place. The doctors would be completely stumped and have to perform an autopsy to determine her cause of death. She grimaced at the thought of having her chest cut open and poked at like some meaningless lab rat. *What would they find?* She wondered. *Wouldn't it be ironic if when they opened her up the lamp was inside?*

Inside of her? Abigail thought about that for a while. The mark burned deeper into her wrist, and the blood began to drip onto her pants. She got up and walked back up to the marketplace. She found a bathroom and wet some paper towels to wash the blood off her pants and arm.

Abigail looked at her face in the mirror. Her fear subsided for a moment and she smiled at her reflection. "Miss St. George, I'm here to grant your wish, what shall it be?" she asked.

Abigail thought carefully, she wanted to make sure she formed her words just right, so there would be no way to turn and twist them around on her. She spoke clearly back to the mirror. "I wish I had been wise enough not to buy the lamp in the first place."

The lights in the small bathroom flickered on and off, and finally went completely black. The room was as small and dark as a closet. Abigail closed her eyes and rubbed her wrist. She took a deep breath and slowly opened them.

"Can I help you find anything?" the man behind the counter in the store asked.

Abigail looked at him, then at the small brass lamp that sat perched in the window display. She started to reach for it, but hesitated. *It wouldn't be a wise purchase. Let the yuppie buy it herself.* She turned and looked at the man. "Got any good chocolate?"

About Sherry

Sherry Briscoe, award-winning author of MISTS OF GARIBALDI: Tales of the Supernatural, and FORGOTTEN LIVES: Where Evil Lurks – the first of the Ninth Miracle Trilogy, is also the founder of the Idaho Screenwriters Association. Board member for the Idaho Writers Guild, she teaches and helps other writers in the community.
www.sherrybriscoe.com

LILY AND THE LAMP

Catherine Valenti

Juliette stopped dusting when her rag hit the brass base of Lily's Aladdin lamp. A shiver zapped her from head to toe. Every time she was around this lamp she had a faint feeling of unease. *Oh, come on, Juliette. There's nothing wrong with the lamp, you just don't like it because it throws off the entire decor of the room.* Not to mention it looked like the type of fixture her great-grandmother would have had. As a child. A century ago.

It was striking though, with its embellished brass base, an old-time translucent pearl globe surrounding the post, and a lampshade with a fringe tail at each panel corner. Lily had fallen in love with the flowers painted on the globe. Roses, daisies, tiny forget-me-nots, and others; in all the colors of the rainbow and then some.

She shook her head as her fingers encircled the lamp and lifted it to dust underneath. It couldn't have been too ancient, since it had an electrical plug and was in pristine condition. There was no manufacturing date anywhere she could see, just a faint etching of "Aladdin Lamp Mfg." along the bottom edge of the brass base.

It was the right size for Lily's nightstand, just over twelve inches in height, from the bottom of the base to the top of the tulip shaped finial that held the shade. Short enough for a five-year-old to turn on and off easily from her bed, yet with room to showcase the bouquets of painted flowers that entranced her youngest daughter.

I guess it was my own fault. Juliette positioned the lamp so the prettiest blooms faced the front. Last weekend they had taken their girls on an outing to an arcade and miniature golf in Sandstone, about an hour away. Driving back, she had noticed a neighborhood yard sale and talked Andrew into stopping.

After a few driveways filled with the usual fare of cast-off clothing, broken dolls, and furniture in need of loving repair, Lily spied the lamp. "Mommy, Mommy, look!" It was in her hands, and that look in Lily's eyes – they sparkled with joy.

Andrew was all over it – and damn it, he encouraged Lily. He was the biggest pushover father there ever was.

"Dear," Juliette had told him, trying to keep her words direct but sweet, since the girls were listening. "It's a cute lamp and all, but this would be so out of place in Lily's room. It's so... so... old."

He hadn't even had time to agree how illogical it would be to bring that lamp home and put it in Lily's room, because the woman running the yard sale was right there, in Juliette's face. "It's a lovely lamp, very old but doesn't it look like brand new? A collector's item for sure," then noting Juliette looking pointedly at her five-year-old holding the antique lamp, she had added, "but it is so sturdy. My own daughter had it for a long time and it is really unbreakable. It's..." At that, the woman's eyes had misted over, and she ran a hand over her face.

Andrew had seemed ready to buy it on the spot. "The price is excellent, Jules," he said. "Lily loves it. One mismatched piece isn't going to ruin her whole bedroom." He had taken the lamp from his daughter and turned it this way and that. "It's been well taken care of."

Juliette caved as Lily gave her that pleading look with those big blue eyes. Even ten-year-old Amanda had sided with her sister. As Juliette dug in her purse for the money, the woman picked up a picture book from the same table and gave it to Lily. "For you, little one. It goes with the lamp, please keep them together. I hope you love it as much as my... my own daughter did."

That, of course, was the *coup de grace* as Lily grabbed the book. She had looked up at the woman, and given her the biggest, toothiest Lily-smile she had. "It's princesses!" she'd cried.

Nothing to be done about it now. Juliette looked down and spied the Princess and the Pony book that went with the lamp. It must have fallen from the bed when Lily climbed out this morning, as it was always tucked in her arms when she fell asleep at night.

Juliette picked it up and thumbed through a few pages. The book smelled of age, and the drawing on the cover seemed to be decades old, yet the interior was pristine. No rips, crayon marks, or even bent pages.

It was a trite, simple story about a little princess with a magic lamp. Juliette held the book closer to her face. The picture inside looked a lot like Lily's lamp. *Great marketing ploy.* The Princess Lorelei, a chubby little darling with hazel eyes and chin-length brown hair, made wishes. Each was granted in a different manner, despite protests by her father and mother, the king and queen. A kitten, the sparkly dress, and of course in the end, the pony. And she lived happily ever after.

Pressure hit the side of her head, and a sudden burst of nausea threatened to spill the contents of her stomach. Juliette left the book by the lamp and stumbled to her own bed. She managed to lay down and cover her eyes before the spinning room could knock her down. Hopefully this migraine would dissipate quickly. She had to pick up Lily soon.

***

"Mommy, do you want to hear the song we learned in school?" Lily skipped alongside Juliette as they walked home from her kindergarten. Autumn leaves blanketed parts of the sidewalk, making a delightful crunch underfoot.

"Of course, Lily." Juliette's head was still foggy, and the

last thing she wanted was noise, but she didn't want to hurt her daughter's feelings.

"*Black and white and spotted paws, and a purple toy between her jaws.*" Lily giggled at her own singing. "I want a puppy with a purple toy." As if that wasn't sufficient, she added, "I want to be a princess with sparkles and I want a puppy with a purple toy."

Juliette smiled despite the continual throb at her temples. At five Lily was enchantingly charming almost all the time. Her daughter was at the age where she fell in love with people and animals in books, songs, and movies.

Once home, Juliette set out lunch for Lily, who sat at her little table intent on her latest coloring project. She grasped the purple crayon in her hand and made arching swipes inside a sketch she'd made of a blob with a head and four legs.

"Is that your puppy?" Juliette asked as she gave Lily a plate holding a sandwich and cut up fruit.

"Yeah," Lily said, finishing a last scribble before lifting her head. "It's my homework. He's purple."

"You have homework in kindergarten, honey?"

Lily nodded. "Just like Manda." She chatted on about her sister, then her teacher, then what happened at the playground. Juliette listened on autopilot as she finished the dishes.

By four o'clock when Amanda came bursting in, Juliette's headache had subsided. Lily bounced up and down as she showed Amanda her drawings – she had added a princess picture to the dog sketch.

Andrew called just as Juliette was taking the chicken out of the oven. "Hi honey, there's a little issue here," he said, and she cringed. When he used that phrase it meant he wouldn't be escaping the office anytime soon.

"Should I keep dinner warm for you?" Hopefully this time the crisis could be resolved quickly, but Juliette wouldn't hold her breath.

"It might take two or three more hours." Andrew's voice

sounded properly apologetic. "I feel bad, but I don't have much of a choice. Can I talk to the girls?"

After hearing how sad Amanda and Lily sounded as they talked to their dad, Juliette's frustration diminished a bit. Her husband did his best, but it was still difficult being a single parent at bedtime, when she was already exhausted.

The girls finished dinner, bathed, and brushed their teeth. Juliette scanned through school bags and made sure all necessary papers were inside for the next day. Her daughters were employing their usual stall tactics in lieu of going to bed.

"Girls, really, it's way past your bedtime," Juliette said, hearing her voice rise a decibel or so. She pressed her lips together and took a deep breath.

"Mom, it's not that late," Amanda said, staring pointedly at the kitchen clock. "What about our stories?"

"Stories, Mommy, stories!" Lily sounded whiny-tired. "The princess story."

"Amanda, Mommy has to clean the kitchen. Can you read one story to Lily tonight?" Her eldest daughter crossed her arms and turned to look at Lily. "Please?"

"I'll read her a story, but can I stay up a little longer? I want to finish my book so I can get another one. It's library day tomorrow. Remember?"

"Fine, but get going," Juliette said. "I'll be there in about ten minutes."

By the time Juliette made it upstairs, she found Amanda with her nose deep in her latest book. "Goodnight sweetie, five more minutes, then lights out."

Juliette peeked through the partially-opened door to Lily's room. Hopefully her littlest angel was sound asleep. No such luck. Juliette could see Lily in profile, standing next to her bed, facing the lamp. Her tiny fingers traced one of the flowers and she was smiling and whispering. The Aladdin lamp glowed, casting shadows behind her daughter.

"Lily, what are you doing?"

Her daughter jumped and swung around, eyes wide.

"Oh sweetie, I didn't mean to startle you, but it's time to go to sleep now." Juliette brushed a strand of hair from her face and came into the room. *Actually, I need to go to sleep now.* It had been a long day, and she was exhausted.

"Okay, Mommy." Lily climbed into her bed and pulled the blanket up to her chin. Her little smile melted Juliette's heart.

"You silly girl, I love you," she whispered to her daughter, brushing blond locks from her forehead. She gave Lily a goodnight kiss, and tried to click off the lamp. The switch moved, but the lamp stayed on. "Odd, this switch seems to be broken." Once more she jiggled the switch, and suddenly the light went off, sending shadows weaving around the room. Lily giggled softly as Juliette made her way to the door.

***

The next morning Andrew fed the girls and made Juliette's coffee while she showered and dressed. "Lucky me," she said as she saw him in front of the sink.

She hugged him, and Andrew wrapped his arms around her and kissed her dramatically. "Anything for you, my darling," he said in a cheesy Italian accent, while Lily and Amanda giggled.

A clear head, a beautiful autumn day, breakfast chores nearly done by her handsome husband, who had promised he would be home early tonight. What more could she want?

The morning flew by. Juliette ticked all her chores off the list except the grocery shopping. *No problem, I'll just drive to the school, and Lily can help me shop.*

Lily talked and giggled as they left the school parking lot. Juliette had just entered the roundabout past Madison Street when in a flash something entered the street. She slammed on the brakes. A small dog, maybe a puppy, had darted in front of her from behind some bushes.

"You okay, Lily?" she asked. Lily was definitely shaken up, and was starting to cry. "It's okay, honey, there was something in the road but we missed it." Juliette pulled over, and stepped out to take a closer look.

"Mommy!" Juliette turned to her daughter, who was straining as far as possible out of her booster seat. "Look, Mommy, it's my puppy!"

The small white dog turned to look at them. It had black patches, floppy ears, and a wagging tail.

"Great," Juliette muttered. "Now what." She looked around hoping to find the owner, but no one was in sight. Just a few cars passing by. The dog bounded toward her.

"Go home, puppy," she said, waving her arms. Didn't do much good, as the puppy jumped up on her. Juliette backed against the driver's door. "No jumping, dog. Go home!"

"Mommy, it's my puppy!" Lily was bouncing up and down in her seat.

"Lily, this dog belongs to someone. See, it's been fed, and it's friendly. We need to let it go back home."

"No," Lily yelled. "It's mine. You can't let her go."

Juliette couldn't leave this animal in the middle of the road. She scooped the dog up and put it in the back seat beside Lily, who was overjoyed.

"Lily," she said, in her sternest voice. "We can't keep this puppy or dog, whatever it is. It has a home, and we need to take it to the dog shelter so the owners can get it back."

"No, Mommy, she's mine." Lily spoke with confidence. "We need to take her home. Her name is Purple."

Juliette just shook her head and drove down the road, every now and then taking a look to the back seat where Lily was stroking and hugging the dog.

Once home, Lily picked up the puppy and attempted to carry it inside. Although the dog was small, so was Lily, and in spite of her irritation at this whole affair, Juliette had to smile. The animal dangled almost to the ground. Lily staggered through the door, determination in each step.

"Really, Lily, we can't keep the dog," Juliette said, watching the puppy lick Lily as she stroked it and murmured baby talk. Lily's lower lip came out, and she narrowed her eyes at her mother.

"Purple needs me, Mommy," she said. "I love her."

It wasn't easy, making the call to the animal shelter with the escapee in question capturing her daughter's heart. The lady who answered the phone wasn't much help, claiming no one had called about a missing puppy. The shelter was very full, and she suggested Juliette bring the puppy in to check for a microchip. She asked if Juliette could keep the dog until they could find the owners. Juliette shook her head even as she muttered a reluctant "yes" and then was stuck when the woman asked if the puppy was male or female and wanted a complete description.

"I don't know," Juliette said, upset now that unless she drew a hard line, the puppy was theirs, at least for awhile. She turned the dog over, who seemed to love the idea of a belly rub, and reported to the clerk that they were looking at a female. "She's young, maybe an older puppy?" Juliette wasn't a dog expert.

After giving her name and contact information and seeking more than one reassurance that she would be called as soon as the owner showed up, Juliette hung up the phone.

"Hmm," Juliette said to both the puppy and her daughter. "Looks like we need to buy dog food and get some blankets out."

Lily hugged her puppy as she smiled up at her mother. "Her name is Purple, remember?" Lily stood up and patted her thigh. "C'mon Purple, let's go to the store." It was such a cute sight. Poor little girl would be heartbroken when the real owner claimed the wayward animal.

As it was, when Juliette informed her the puppy would have to stay in the utility room while they went shopping, big tears formed in Lily's eyes.

"I want Purple to come with us!"

"Honey, she can't stay in the car by herself," then anticipating the response before Lily could voice it, "and you can't be in the car without a grownup."

Lily squatted down and patted Purple on the head. "Don't worry, we'll be back soon." Then she kissed the puppy right on her mouth.

"Lily, no!" Juliette wrinkled up her face. "Don't put your mouth on the dog. You don't know what it's been rolling in. Eww."

Her daughter ignored her, and ran past her to the door. "Mommy, we need to hurry and come back so she won't be alone."

***

Amanda came home after soccer practice, her cleats tapping on the floor.

"Shoes off," Juliette said automatically, and almost fell as the dog burst past her to greet Amanda.

"Oh, who is this?" Amanda squealed, kneeling and taking sloppy kisses. Right in the face. Juliette grimaced.

She started saying something about a stray when Lily flew through the door to her sister. "She's the puppy I wanted. Her name is Purple!"

Amanda stood quickly, and looked from her sister to Juliette. "You got a puppy?"

Lily nodded happily.

"No, she did not get a puppy," Juliette said. "This dog ran out in front of us by the school. It's a stray, and we're taking it in tomorrow so the shelter can find its owner."

Amanda's face turned ashen, and her eyes opened wide. She took a step back.

"Honey, what's wrong? You look like you've seen a ghost." Juliette said. Lily and the dog ran out of the kitchen into the back yard.

"We're not keeping it?"

"Just overnight. Tell me what's going on with you?"

Amanda shook her head. "Nothing." She grabbed her book bag and hurried from the room. Juliette could hear her cleats on the stairs.

"Take off your shoes!" she called after her daughter.

***

When Andrew arrived home, he was greeted by both Lily and the puppy. "Her name is Purple, and she's my dog," Lily declared.

Juliette had warned him in advance, and he had not been pleased. The dog circled around him, wagging her tail, before following Lily outside. At least the dog had the good sense not to jump on Andrew.

"Really?" he said, putting down his laptop case, and taking off his jacket. "The dog has a name? And treats? And toys?" He couldn't miss the pile of dog goodies on the table.

"She is a cutie, isn't she?" Juliette said, a little hesitantly. "I'm sure she has an owner. We can take her in tomorrow to check for a microchip so they can track down her family."

"We are not keeping her, Jules," he said, watching Lily and Purple chase each other in the yard. One side of his mouth lifted. He was trying not to smile.

When Juliette called the family to the table for dinner, she had to remind Lily that Purple needed to stay out of the dining room. Then Andrew reminded her they shouldn't be naming the dog, since it was not staying. Purple lay in the corner, head on her paws, acting like a perfect angel as she watched the family sit down.

Halfway through the meal, Juliette noticed Amanda was unusually quiet. She had been acting odd since she saw the dog. As soon as dinner was over Amanda asked to be excused and went to her room. Andrew must have noticed her odd behavior too, and they exchanged a puzzled look.

"I'll go talk to her," Juliette said. Andrew had Lily help him clear the table and wash dishes.

Juliette knocked on her daughter's door. "Can we talk?"

She heard Amanda's quiet yes, and opened the door. Her daughter sat at her desk, staring absently at her math book.

"Are you upset about the dog? You've been so quiet since you came home."

Amanda shook her head, avoiding her mother's gaze.

"It's not Lily's. She's a stray, and I'm sure the owners will be looking for her."

"No, they won't," Amanda said. She finally looked up at Juliette. "It's not the dog. The dog is fine. It's just that Lily...

she... she wished the dog here. Whatever she wishes for, she gets."

A strange chill passed through Juliette's body. Amanda sat with shoulders hunched, trembling slightly. She was definitely upset, maybe envious?

"Amanda, your sister doesn't get everything she wants. You know that."

"Not everything she *wants*," Amanda said. "Everything she..."

Juliette waited, but her daughter was done talking. Amanda turned back to her book and stuck music buds in her ears.

As Juliette closed the door behind her, she frowned. This was not like her daughter. Hopefully Amanda would be back to her normal, cheery self in the morning.

***

Lily and Juliette were taking advantage of their free time. Lily was out of kindergarten for the afternoon, and Juliette had several hours left before she needed to pick up Amanda from school. They arrived at Costume Emporium shortly after noon. Halloween was only two weeks away, Lily had reminded her. Amanda's costume would be difficult, as usual, since she refused to buy one. She loved custom-made creations, so it was always a challenge. Lily's was easier – she would be Princess Lily. Juliette thought the theme itself would make things easy, but the actual costume shopping proved challenging. Turned out Lily was extremely selective, especially for a five-year-old.

"No," Lily said, tossing aside the first one with silvery glitters and faux diamonds embedded in the tiara. She also nixed the pink princess-style gown with a golden scepter.

When she saw the lavender gown, with dark-purple beads sewn throughout, she was finally done shopping. At that point Juliette had stopped looking at price tags, figuring any costume would be worth the price in order to escape the store with the perfect Princess Lily outfit.

Lily didn't release her gown, not when the cashier had to

search for the price tag, not when she carried it to the car, and not when she stepped out and took it into her room. She put it on, glided to the kitchen, swirled for Juliette's benefit, and announced "It's so pretty!"

"You are beautiful," Juliette said. Lily's face glowed with joy as she danced around the kitchen. Purple jumped around and danced with her. *I can't believe the dog is still here, but I admit, she's sweet.*

After more than a week with no one claiming Purple, Andrew had finally admitted defeat. Even Amanda, who in the first few days wouldn't even look at the dog, had warmed to her.

"Mommy, I wish I was a princess."

"You are a princess, a beautiful purple princess," Juliette said. She knelt down and brushed Lily's hair out of her face.

Her daughter shook her head. "A real princess, Mommy. I wish I was a real one."

Juliette smiled. "You are very real to me, sweetie. Now, Miss Princess, it's time to change out of your royal gown so we can take Purple on her walk."

Lily scampered to her room, the dog at her heels.

Later that evening, Juliette and Andrew snuggled together on the sofa. She laid her head on his shoulder. "Don't you think our lives are picture-perfect?"

He drew her closer, and gave her a kiss.

The sound of barking and howling pierced the house. Juliette jumped up, following Andrew who took the stairs two at a time.

Amanda stood like a statue just inside Lily's room, her back against the wall. Lily was next to the bed, facing the glowing Aladdin lamp, not moving. Purple pushed up against her, whining, and looking up at the light.

"Lily?" Andrew scooped her up as Juliette rushed over. Their little daughter blinked a few times, and gazed slowly around the room.

"I think she's sleepwalking," Juliette said. Lily wrapped her arms around Andrew and her eyes closed.

Andrew frowned, and he gently laid her back in her bed. Purple jumped up, and snuggled in next to Lily. Juliette covered her up and they both peered at their daughter. She was sound asleep, her breathing soft and slow.

Juliette clicked off the lamp, and she and Andrew turned to the door. Amanda still stood at the entry, her eyes wide. Juliette embraced her, then led her back to bed. "It's okay, Lily was dreaming or something."

"Good thing the dog warned us. She could have tumbled down the stairs," Andrew said.

***

For the second time that night, Purple roused the family with her barking and growling. Juliette and Andrew sprang up at the same time. Their room was dark, lit only by the glowing red 2:07 on the digital display of the clock radio.

She half-stumbled down the hall, right behind Andrew who had flipped on the light. He pushed Lily's door open. The Aladdin lamp glowed, and Purple snarled and whined in front of it.

Lily's bedding was rumpled, but she wasn't in it. "Lily?" she called. Andrew hurried to the window, while she opened the sliding closet doors. Purple growled, then broke into a series of howls. "Where's Lily?"

Andrew joined Juliette on the floor, looking under the bed. As they stood, she saw Amanda by the door, looking shaken. "Mom? Dad? What's going on?"

"Lily's not in her room," Juliette said. *Was she sleepwalking again?* "We need to find her."

"What's that dog doing? What the hell is she barking at?" Andrew looked at Amanda. "Get her out of here, take her with you back to your room."

Amanda stepped slowly toward Purple. "Come here, girl," she said, her voice trembling. Purple slunk to Amanda, looking back once and whining, before following her from the room.

Juliette and Andrew searched every room, every closet, every cabinet. They checked the doors and all the windows.

All of them were still closed and locked. Andrew went through the garage, and walked around outside.

When Juliette checked on Amanda, her daughter was curled up in her bed, Purple right next to her. They were both trembling. Juliette tried to comfort her daughter, but her own terror seemed to make things worse.

She went back down the stairs. Andrew was still opening cabinets in the kitchen. Her heart was pounding, and there was a rushing noise in her head. *Where was Lily?*

***

It had been twelve days since Lily disappeared, seemingly into thin air. Andrew finally went back to work, and Amanda to school. No one talked to each other much. There didn't seem to be anything new to say.

Detectives called once a day, but after the first week, stopped asking Juliette and Andrew to come in for questioning. Friends from church and the girls' school stopped by with cards, food, and words of encouragement. The local search and rescue group scoured the nearby fields, and the police went around the neighborhood, knocking on doors and looking for any clues at all.

For a time, Juliette knew she and Andrew were suspects in Lily's disappearance, because there seemed to be no other possibilities. All the doors and windows were secure, there were no broken branches or footprints in the garden beds bordering the house, and zero signs of forced entry. Their baby had simply vanished.

Migraines attacked her every day, and the drugs she brought home from the pharmacy barely touched the pain. Mostly they caused her to wander around the house, lost, a thick cloud of confusion and sorrow choking her.

She managed to pull herself together to leash up Purple and walk to the school every day to meet Amanda. No way would she take a chance on losing a second daughter.

On this day, Juliette found herself in Lily's room, lying on the bed as she often did. Eyes closed, wishing Lily back. She heard a quiet knock on the door and opened her eyes to see

Amanda watching her from the threshold.

"Mom?" Amanda's voice was tentative, hushed.

Juliette struggled to sit up. "What is it Amanda?"

"You need to see something." She held a section of the Sunday newspaper in her hand. Juliette had stopped reading papers, or even going online after the first few days. It was too difficult.

"It's in the paper. This girl was found. In her home. She'd been gone a year, and everyone thought she was dead."

At this Juliette motioned her daughter closer. "Let me see."

The story ran in the human interest section of the paper, with the headline "Child Thought Dead Found Safe."

She scanned the article – six-year-old Sara Bell had disappeared, just over a year ago. No signs of struggle, few clues, she disappeared into thin air, or so they thought at first. A few weeks later the police arrested a man who lived on their street, and a few months after that he was convicted of her kidnapping, and suspected of murdering her although her body was never recovered. Almost two weeks ago little Sara was discovered in her own bedroom, apparently unhurt.

Juliette let out a gasp, and started in on the article again, reading it slowly and carefully.

The convicted kidnapper, Hal Jenkins, had done some remodeling work for the Bell family, so was familiar with the layout of their house and yard. Jenkins' rap sheet was "a mile long" according to detectives. Burglary, armed robbery, kidnapping, drugs, and sexual abuse of a minor.

The Bells lived in Sandstone, a small town about thirty miles from their home in Riverside. Sara had been safely tucked into bed at night, and was gone the next morning. Investigators failed to find any sign of forced entry. During their neighborhood canvass, they found a child's shoe in Jenkins' front yard that turned out to be Sara's. After obtaining a search warrant, they found child pornography on his computer, more children's shoes, and several pairs of underwear, one of which contained the missing girl's DNA.

Jenkins admitted to stealing the items from around the neighborhood, but vehemently denied kidnapping Sara Bell. Her parents made a public statement expressing their sorrow over the loss of their daughter, and included a message of forgiveness for the man who had been convicted of the murder and kidnapping of Sara.

Three months after his incarceration, Jenkins was found dead, an apparent suicide by hanging.

Eleven days ago Sara was found by her mother. She was asleep in her bed. Despite multiple interviews, and even a session with a hypnotist, Sara could not remember where she had been, insisting she fell asleep the previous night and woke up as usual the next morning. Doctors examined her and declared her healthy with no signs of physical trauma of any kind. This mystery stumped everyone.

Word spread about this remarkable story, and although Sara's parents tried to avoid publicity, they had no choice but to give a short statement to the media thanking those involved in the search, and asking for privacy for their family. The police department stated they would reopen the case, since either Jenkins was not involved, or there were other parties to this kidnapping.

"We need to show this to your dad." Juliette met her daughter's gaze. Both had tears in their eyes. Sudden realization hit her. How terrifying this must be for Amanda, such a young girl to be brought into such a horror. *I haven't been much of a mother to her lately.* She put her arms around her daughter and hugged her. "It will be okay."

Amanda took a step back. She sniffed and wiped tears from her eyes. "There's more Mom," she said. "Look at the picture of Sara Bell."

Juliette studied the photo. A smiling little girl with chubby cheeks and short dark hair. Where had she seen this girl before?

"Mom?"

Juliette looked up, brow furrowed, frowning.

"Mom, she looks like Princess Lorelei in Lily's book."

"Where's that book?" Juliette looked around the room. Lily had always kept it close to her in the bed, now it was gone. Amanda rummaged through the books on the shelf.

"Here it is," she said as she brought it over. They opened the book and sat in horrified silence.

It was Lily. The princess was Lily.

***

The three of them sat around the kitchen table. Dinner was untouched, and cold.

"What do you think happened?" Juliette looked from Andrew to Amanda.

Andrew spoke first. "Our daughter disappeared the same morning Sara Bell appeared safely back home. I read that book to her, so many times..." He lowered his head and drew a few deep breaths. "The girl in the book didn't look like Lily at all. Now she does. How?"

The past few days had been a blur. None of them could come up with any logical way to tell the police what they suspected. They couldn't prove the princess in the book had changed from Sara to Lily, and, as Juliette pointed out, there were several publishers who would use a child's likeness in their stories to personalize them. The police would think they had all gone mad.

"The Aladdin lamp," Amanda said. "I caught her making wishes with it. And I tried to tell you," her voice was shaking, "Lily made wishes, and told them to the lamp. They came true."

"The dog?" Andrew asked.

Their daughter nodded. "Purple. And other things. Little things, like new crayons and the sparkly bracelet. Maybe you didn't see them, but I did."

"Why didn't you say something before?" Juliette asked.

"It was the lamp. You wouldn't have believed me."

Juliette's gaze went to Andrew, but he was staring at Amanda. "We need to destroy the lamp," he said, venom in his voice.

"We can't," Juliette said. "It might be the only way back

for Lily."

"It's an Aladdin lamp," Amanda said. "In every story I read about it, the genie grants wishes. Maybe we could wish her back."

Juliette and Andrew turned to stare at their daughter, then glanced at each other. In silence they all stood, Juliette picked up the book, and they climbed the stairs toward Lily's room. Purple followed, whining quietly.

Once there, they were at a loss. Amanda composed herself, took the book from Juliette and stopped in front of the lamp. She reached for the switch. Juliette realized she was holding her breath, and tried to let it out softly. The lamp lit, and Amanda stared at it.

Now what? Juliette wished she had some answers.

Amanda touched the painted flowers, and traced them with her fingers. Juliette took in a quick breath, and held it.

"I wish..." Amanda turned to look at her parents, then back at the lamp. "I wish Lily would come out of the book and be back home with us."

Silence. Nothing. No Lily. The lamp went dark and Juliette heard screaming. Her own screams.

Andrew put his arms around Amanda and Juliette and rushed them out of the room, closing the door securely once Purple had followed them out.

They huddled together, not daring to go back in.

"Where did we get the lamp?" Andrew said, breaking the silence. "Who sold it to us? We need to find that person."

"Oh, my God! It was her," Juliette said. "In Sandstone at the yard sale. It was Sara Bell's mother who sold it to us."

***

Juliette turned off the car, and again read the numbers on the house to her left. Six. Zero. Eight. Nine. Five. She glanced at the scribble on her paper. This was Lydia Bell's house. Sara's mother.

Two weeks had passed since Amanda tried unsuccessfully to bring Lily home. Fourteen days of tears, arguments, accusations, and sorrow. Two days ago Juliette searched public records for the Bell home. After a few dead ends and the use of her credit card, she finally found it.

At first Andrew was nervous, insisting that trying to talk to Lydia Bell would be a waste of time. She had her daughter back, she would want to bury the past. Why would she admit the truth?

And what was the truth, exactly? Sara Bell was in the book, now Lily was in the book. The lamp was sentient? Capable of most horrifying, evil deeds? Nothing they tried in the past fourteen days had brought their baby back. Each day their hearts broke a little more, and each moment that passed Juliette felt herself losing her grasp on reality.

I just need to breathe, Juliette told herself. She picked up the princess book, opened the car door, and hesitated before walking slowly up the sidewalk. This wasn't easy. It was, however, necessary. She – they – needed their baby back.

Her finger pushed the doorbell. Once, twice, and then she forced herself to stop. Her mouth was so dry, how could she hope to form words?

There was no answer, so she knocked. Hard. From the corner of her eye Juliette noticed a flutter in the curtains covering a window by the door.

"Mrs. Bell, please open the door! My name is Juliette, and I really need to talk to you about this book and my daughter." She held the book up, toward the fluttering curtains.

Finally the door opened slowly. Juliette resisted the urge to burst in. Sara's mother stood in front of her.

"Who are you? What do you want?"

"My name is Juliette."

"You told me. What do you want?" Lydia Bell sounded almost defiant. Yet there was something else... a bit of fear in her eyes. That's when Juliette took a step back.

"You!" Juliette said, and now she was certain. "You – you sold us the lamp. The book. This book!" She held it up in front of her. "You're Lydia Bell. You knew. You knew!"

Lydia took a step back and reached for the door. At the

same time, Juliette moved forward and entered the house. "You have to talk to me. You have to tell me. My daughter Lily is missing. She's in here. This book. It was Sara before. Now it's Lily!"

"I d-don't know. Go away. We didn't do anything." Lydia's eyes were wide, she held both hands out in front of her.

Juliette felt tears threatening. "I'm not here to hurt you. I just need to know... to know how we can get Lily back."

Lydia Bell stared at Juliette. There was so much sorrow in those eyes. She looked down at the book Juliette held open in front of her. Princess Lorelei was now Lily.

Finally Lydia met Juliette's gaze, and held it for several minutes. "Come in," she said. "I'm so sorry. So sorry."

They sat in gray and maroon arm chairs, facing each other in silence until Lydia broke it.

"No one would believe it. I didn't myself at first." Her voice broke, and she clenched her hands together. "Sara fell in love with that lamp as soon as she saw it. It was in an antique shop in Meyerville. It was her birthday. That was one of her presents. The book came with it – the owner insisted. He told us the book went with the lamp. They were not to be separated. They couldn't be."

Juliette listened in horror as Lydia described the same familiar scenarios – Sara entranced by the lamp, tracing its designs. How she wished for certain things, and they were granted. She wanted a cat – and the next day one ended up on their doorstep. Sara cried because she was an only child – a week later, on a whim and due to unexplained nausea – Lydia took a test and discovered she was pregnant. More odd things happened, and the longer it went on, the more Lydia, and finally her husband, connected Sara's obsession with the lamp to the 'coincidences'.

One night while Sara slept, they threw the lamp and the book in the trash. The next morning it was back by her bed, and somehow their daughter knew.

"She told us," Lydia said, a few tears running down her

eyes. "We could never throw the lamp away. She wished she was the princess in the book. Then she would have the lamp always. Always." She sat up straight, took a deep breath. "The next day she was gone. A few months later, when we were going through her things one more time, we saw her. In the book."

Lydia's eyes, full of sorrow, but also with a hint of determination, looked straight at Juliette.

Juliette drew back in horror. "You knew! You made us take the lamp, and the book. You knew!"

"I tried many times, but the right girl never came along. When your daughter picked up the lamp, I knew. Or at least I finally had hope. I'm sorry for your girl, but I would do it again to get my Sara back."

***

It was their tenth yard sale. They held their first five only a week apart, until the president of the homeowners association paid them a personal visit to let them know they had complaints from neighbors about their frequency.

After the first time, Juliette realized they didn't have enough junk to draw anyone in, so they spent every free day buying up odds and ends from want ads and other people's sales. Each week, then each month, they advertised. It cost big money to buy the kind of items that drew families in – they concentrated on clothes, toys, books, and furniture that would appeal to five-year-old girls. Amanda contributed, designing her own jewelry made of colorful beads – necklaces and bracelets, little toe rings and gaudy, sparkly pieces sewn on headbands and belts.

***

The sun beat down, and Juliette reached a hand up to wipe the sweat. Her hand stopped mid-air. She spotted them almost immediately. Dad had wild red hair that flew out above his ears. He carried a young boy in his arms, a spitting genetic image. Mom sported a ponytail, and dangly earrings, and she held the hand of another redhead. A little girl, maybe five or six years old.

Juliette watched as Amanda led the girl to the table with all the sparklies. Pointed to the book, then put the little girl's hand on the lamp. The Aladdin lamp with roses, daisies, and forget-me-nots of all the colors in the rainbow. And then some.

Andrew stepped up beside his wife, put his arm around her waist. Held her tightly. "This might be it, honey."

Juliette rested her head against Andrew's shoulder, but never took her eyes off the redheaded girl. She felt pounding in her chest. "I have a good feeling about that one."

About Catherine

Catherine Valenti has worked as a freelance editor and ghostwriter for several years. Prior to starting her own business, she wrote educational newsletter articles, business plans, and grant proposals for several different not-for-profit organizations.

Her latest short story is included in *The Ancient*, an anthology by authors known as the Seven. She has several other stories in progress, is working on a novella for the Seven to be released later in 2015, and has a novel ready to edit for future publication.

Cathy lives in Meridian, Idaho, where in addition to writing, she enjoys hiking, running, skiing, and dancing.

REACTION

Bobbi Carol

Law III: To every action there is always opposed an equal reaction: or the mutual actions of two bodies upon each other are always equal, and in opposite directions.

Isaac Newton, Physicist

His beard was short and neatly trimmed. She loved caressing his face, feeling the soft hair under her fingers. She loved kissing those lips.
She felt his hands slowing making their way up her back. Her knees sank deeper into the couch cushion as she straddled him. Felt his need inside her now.
His hands had found her breasts. Fingertips brushed against her nipples...
"Give it to me Liz..."
She kissed the words off his lips – tasted his desire.
She arched her back – pushing harder, deeper.
But the white light was so bright.
Brighter.
Followed by the horrible crushing sound of metal on metal.
She heard herself scream.

The radio woke her.

It's 6:00 – weather and a traffic check are next here on the Buzz Morning Show. But first a few words from our sponsors...

It was only a dream.
Only it wasn't.

Today marked the five year anniversary of the accident. Five years since life had taken away the one man who ever mattered to her. They had only been married nine months. She knew she'd never get over it.

A tear trickled down her face.

Laughter came bounding down the hall, rising in volume, and soon a thirty-five-pound boy-rocket came hurtling into her bed. Wiping away the tears with the back of her hand, she greeted her precocious child with kisses.

"Mama?"

"Yes, my love?"

"Can we get ice cream on the way home today?"

"Ice cream?! It's six in the morning and you are thinking about ice cream?"

"Yes mama. I love ice cream!"

"I know you do baby – and yes, we can stop and get ice cream on the way home today. Now go get your jammies off and get ready. We need to get moving."

***

She dropped Jeremy safely at daycare.

The soothing swish of the windshield wipers combined with the heat inside the car made her wish for her warm bed.

It is going to be another drencher today across the Midstate. The rain will continue throughout the day at a rate of one to two inches per hour. Some minor flooding has begun in lower lying areas. The river is projected to crest sometime tonight around twenty-seven feet. This could cause more serious flooding sooner than expected. Remember to never drive through standing water. You're listening to WBZZ – Buzz 100.

"God, I wish this rain would stop."

Did I say that out loud? Liz wondered.

At least the cemetery was on a hill, so Liz wasn't worried about standing water up here.

Leaving her umbrella in the car, Liz grabbed the flowers she'd brought with her, and made her way down the row of headstones.

Daniel Lee Dodd

THE ANCIENT

March 2, 1983 – April 16, 2009
Devoted Husband

She laid the bouquet next to the marker. Tracing the engraved words with her fingers, her tears mixed with the rain spilling down her face. Not caring how wet she got, she sank down to the ground, stretched her hands wide and hugged the soaked grass.

"Daniel, I miss you so much!"

If only she could hug him for real, feel his lips on hers again.

Her finger touched something soft. Looking up, she realized there was a cloth pouch lying at the base of the headstone.

Swinging from it were a pair of tiny feet.

"What the hell?"

She sat up quickly and shook her head. She must be seeing things. When she looked back, there was indeed a tiny little man sitting on the pouch looking at her.

She was standing and ready to run by the time he spoke.

"Good morning. You have released me from my prison. I must give you a gift in gratitude." His voice was deeper, stronger than it should have been considering his size.

"Released? Gift? Gratitude? What the hell?! Is this some kind of joke?"

"I was imprisoned in that rock", the little man said, pointing to a smooth round stone about the size of a baseball, buried in the grass near the headstone.

"Your caress released me. Now I must repay you – it is our way."

"Our way? Whose way? Caress? Are you some kind of genie? Let me guess: I get three wishes, and no wishing for more wishes?" she said with a smirk.

She needed some coffee, and dry clothes. All this rain was getting to her. Tiny little men offering gifts?

Hallucinations triggered by caffeine withdrawal seemed more likely.

Stumbling, she made her way back to the car.

Apparently he was no hallucination, because there he was again. On the edge of the pavement, leaning on her tire.

"I cannot let you leave without your gift, my lady." His voice rumbled with determination.

She looked at him, hard. He wasn't budging.

"Fine," she said with resignation. "Let's have it before I get any wetter."

Pushing the pouch towards her, he gestured for her to pick it up.

She did, and found the material soft, and although it was still raining hard, and puddles were everywhere, the outside of the pouch remained dry.

"Open it," he commanded.

Pulling apart the drawstring, she tilted it and out rolled three tiny smooth pebbles. They felt warm to the touch. Inviting.

"My gift to you," stated the little man, puffing his chest out with pride.

"Great, just what I was hoping for – three pebbles."

"These are not just pebbles. These pebbles possess the power to grant whatever you desire. All you have to do is speak it aloud."

"Soooo, what? I just say 'I Wish--"

"No, no, no! Stop!" he shouted. His voice boomed, and Liz looked around to see if anyone heard. But there was no one nearby.

"Do not say those words while the pebbles are in your possession, for if you do, whatever you utter next will come to pass. But remember, every time you make a wish, and it is granted, the exact opposite happens somewhere else."

"Why? Are not wishes free? What kind of genie are you?"

"I am not a genie, nor a jinn. I am a ghul. I was imprisoned, and you released me. I have given you your gift. Take it and go, for I am hungry, and you look tasty."

With that, he turned into a cat, and disappeared into the rain.

The rain. Three days of rain was getting old.

Sliding behind the wheel, Liz closed the door and took a second look at the three little pebbles before placing them back in the pouch, and placing it in her pocket.

Flipping the visor down, she combed through her wet hair and used tissues to wipe down her face. It did little good. Trickles of water still found their way down the back of her neck.

She was soaked.

"God, I wish this rain and flooding would stop."

The air crackled. Her pocket felt warm, and the rain stopped. Just stopped. Didn't taper off to a light mist, just stopped.

The sun shone brightly. Puddles began to shrivel and disappear.

"Wait! That wasn't really a wish!" she shouted.

Silence.

"I didn't mean it."

Nothing.

She glanced to her right, and thought she might have seen a cat, weaving its way between the headstones, but she could not be sure.

Sighed.

Liz reached into her pocket. One pebble was missing, just as she'd guessed.

"Damn, well, at least I still have two."

She started the car and headed towards work.

Soft music on the radio returned her thoughts to Daniel, and dancing.

And kissing.

Beep Beep Beep

We interrupt this regularly scheduled program with some breaking news. We are receiving unconfirmed reports of a rare earthquake off the coast of New Jersey. The quake triggered a small tsunami. Early reports state a wall of water ten feet high crashed into the popular boardwalk on the Jersey Shore, causing flooding and major damage. Thankfully the tourist season has not officially started, but at least two are confirmed dead at this time. Locally, the river has suddenly stopped rising as the rain unexpectedly stopped, and the threat of flooding seems to have passed, at least for now. Stay with Buzz Radio. After the break we'll talk to meteorologist Luke Flanners for his take on these developments.

Wait, what?

She shook her head and turned the volume up, but a commercial for a local tire shop had already begun.

"You can trust us to keep you on the road."

Punching the scan button, she searched for more information, maybe a news station.

Reports are still coming in about an unexpected tsunami that hit the Jersey Shore this morning. Sources state it followed an unusual earthquake, and most of the famous boardwalk has suffered extensive damage. Our own Wink reporter, Noah Bull is on the scene.

"Good morning Rick, I spoke to Paula Mealy, director of the West Coast / Alaska Tsunami Warning Center in Palmer, Alaska just moments ago via phone. She has confirmed a tsunami type wave did indeed impact the Jersey Shore this morning at 7:46 am. Currently the rumor this was instigated by an earthquake has not been confirmed by the United States Geological Survey, but there may have been some other source, possibly a subsea slump in the continental shelf along the coastline. She emphasized she has no further information at this time, as it is early in the investigation."

"Were you able to confirm if there were any casualties Noah?"

"Yes, Rick, two people have been confirmed dead, and several more are still missing."

"Thanks Noah, we will hope for the best."

"Absolutely, Rick. We have been told the Governor is expected to make a statement in about an hour. We've been promised more information at that time."

Well folks, that's all we know for now. Please stay tuned to Wink Watch News, we'll bring you the Governor live, and continue to update you as information becomes available.

The ghul's words repeated in Liz's ears: "*But remember this – every time you make a wish, and are granted that wish, the exact opposite will happen somewhere else.*"

Staring dumbfounded at her radio, Liz prayed this wasn't a result of her wish. It couldn't be, could it?

If not, the morning's events were a heck of a coincidence.

***

Two days had passed since the strange little man appeared in Liz's life.

No one understood what made the rain stop that day. The mystery was the hot topic of discussion on all the media outlets.

Not only had it made local news headlines, it had received national attention, on shows such as Today and Good Morning America.

The Midstate would have been flooded, everyone agreed. What happened or how they were spared remained puzzling. The sudden stop to the rain was only one aspect. The river had receded from flood stage more rapidly than could be naturally explained.

Naturally.

That's the word they used. If not naturally, then the conclusion had to be supernatural.

A megachurch downtown was crediting its prayer vigil, taking place at the same time, with moderate success.

Liz suspected, no, was certain of the truth.

But told no one.

A total of five people had lost their lives in the tsunami type wave that came in onto the Jersey Shore. No earthquake had been detected. Scientists couldn't find any evidence of a subsea slump either. There appeared to be no logical explanation.

People were calling it a freak of nature.

Liz just felt guilty.

***

The fifth day dawned bright and sunny, promising a warm and lovely spring weekend.

Liz smiled and watched her son Jeremy playing in the front yard with their dog Charlie.

She couldn't believe how much the boy looked like

Daniel. The same sandy hair, the same soft, gentle, soulful blue eyes. Those same eyes haunted her dreams every night.

Daniel had never gotten to meet his son.

Liz didn't find out she was pregnant until the night of the accident.

The truck driver was drunk, and talking on his phone.

The state trooper had told Liz Daniel had turned the car at the last second, so his side took the brunt of the impact. The officer probably told her with the intent of making her feel better.

It didn't.

Daniel would have been an awesome dad, she was sure.

Right now, she was satisfied to just watch Jeremy throwing the ball.

And Charlie running full tilt chasing it.

Back and forth – neither tiring of the game or each other.

She loved how Charlie had become such an important part of their little family. Who knew, when she rescued him three years ago, he was really rescuing them.

Well, mainly her, from the deep pool of sorrow into which she had descended.

Jeremy had been almost two. They'd stopped to get some pumpkins, and of course, ice cream at a local produce stand.

There were puppies for sale.

They had no papers, were no special breed. The owner couldn't even tell her for sure what kind of dog Charlie was, other than his mom was the tiny little Shih Tzu he had been nursing from.

Charlie was the runt, barely bigger than the palm of her hand, but with a few sideways glances and a shower of kisses, their fate was sealed.

Two weeks later, they brought him home, this little brown and white ball of fur that stole their hearts.

The first night, Liz had almost sat on him while getting him in and out of his crate. He was that tiny. His little yelp did her in, and changed her heart forever.

To say he was a perfect dog would be an understatement.

Crate trained within two weeks.

House trained within a month.

He never chewed on anything but his toys, and he never had accidents.

He rarely barked and never got them up earlier than 6:00 am.

Everyone loved him, and wanted to take him home.

All his wet kisses and cuddles since were mere tools in the world of comfort Charlie bestowed upon them.

With the warm sun, and Jeremy and Charlie having such a good time, Liz thought about how much Daniel would have loved this morning. He would have been content to sit in the sun with her, holding her hand, just watching.

Lord, how she wished she had the energy of her four year old!

Right now, all she wanted to do was lie here, in the warmth of the sun.

And close her eyes.

***

The organ started to play the wedding march.

She looked at her dad, who looked just as scared as she was.

He winked at her as if to say, "We've got this kid…"

Whose bright idea was it to have a wedding in the middle of July? In a church with no air conditioning.

Well, that would have been her. She smiled, thinking back.

July 4th, the day she met Daniel…

"Can I buy you a drink or do you just want the money?"

"Excuse me?"

"Well, I'd like to buy you a drink, but I'm afraid you may be way out of my league, so should I just leave the money here on the bar and call it a day?"

Dimples. That's all she saw, and those beautiful blue eyes.

"Er…um…" She knew she looked and sounded like a complete idiot.

She couldn't stop staring.

If ever there was a perfect specimen of a man.

He was well built and stood about six-one. His jeans did nothing to hide his masculinity, and she could easily see the shape of his muscles through his shirt. Yet he was neither intimidating nor uninviting.

Quite the opposite.

His mouth turned up in a cheesy little smile ending in two dimples that made her heart stop. And he was still smiling.

Waiting for an answer.

"Well, how about you buy me a drink, and we will see if you have to leave money… later."

Did that sound dumb? That sounded dumb.

Sighing.

He probably thought that sounded dumb.

He laughed.

Is that a good sign?

"Hi! I'm Daniel, and you are?"

"Elizabeth." She squeaked.

Did she really just *squeak*?

"Well, Liz. Most people call me Liz, at least friends do. My friends usually call me Liz, unless you prefer to call me Elizabeth. Most people, I mean my friends, they don't…"

Wow, she was rambling.

"I certainly hope we can be friends, *Liz*," he said, smiling even wider.

Was that possible?

The next thing she knew, she'd invited him to her parent's house for a picnic the next day. No more than three hours after she had met him.

What was she thinking?

She was thinking about those dimples, and those jeans that fit just right.

That's what she was thinking.

After a day filled with hot dogs, hamburgers, and lawn games, they had ended the evening back at her apartment, finally falling asleep around 2:00 in the morning.

THE ANCIENT

She had never done that before.

She was always cautious, played hard to get.

She couldn't even remember the last guy she'd allowed to come home with her.

This time was different.

Daniel was different.

She knew she loved him inside of a week. He would tell her later he knew the first time he laid eyes on her.

She didn't know if she quite believed him, but he could make her believe anything.

There was a week of marathon late night phone conversations.

There were the dates that turned into all nighters, then all weekers, and eventually he never went home.

Three months later she asked him to marry her.

Yeah, it's not normally done that way, but she didn't care. She wanted him to be hers and hers alone, forever.

He said yes, and surprised her with a beautiful ring right then and there.

Apparently he had already planned on asking her.

Funny how nerves get in the way.

And now, there he was standing at the front of the church.

With that silly grin on his face – and those dimples.

God, she loved those dimples!

The music.

The dancing.

The laughter.

It was a perfect day.

And they had the rest of their lives to—

***

She woke with a start.

Did she really fall asleep?

Where was Jeremy?

Looking at her phone – she realized it had only been ten minutes, but it had felt like hours.

As she was trying to refocus her brain and come back to

reality, two things happened simultaneously.

First, she heard Jeremy scream something that sounded like Charlie's name.

Secondly, she heard Charlie make a sound. A low, quavering miserable noise that sounded like a cross between a whine and a whimper, followed by a little yelp.

Springing from her chair in an awkward movement combining tangled limbs and plastic, she turned towards the sounds, only to see the splatter of blood and fur in the middle of the street.

"Chaaaar—leeeee!" The word came out in two long syllables of agonizing fear trailing behind her as she ran to the street.

She couldn't deal with this. Not Charlie. Not now, not today.

Kneeling over Charlie lying in the street, she cried. Great whole body wracking sobs filled with grief and despair.

Jeremy was inconsolable.

"I'm sorry mama! I threw the ball too far..." He sobbed, looking down at the dog. "What's wrong with Charlie mama?"

His face.

Tears were streaming down, mixing with the dirt and making tracks. Dripping onto his shirt. Her favorite shirt too. Blue – like his eyes.

Blue with little brown wet circles.

She grabbed him and pulled him close.

"Oh baby, oh honey, it's not your fault!"

How could she comfort him when she felt none herself?

She had to find a way.

"Hush baby."

"It will be alright."

"Charlie..." she whispered, the desperation evident in her voice. "It will be alright. You will be alright, please be alright..."

Holding Jeremy with one hand, Charlie's head in her lap, she softly stroked his fur with her other, trying her best to comfort him.

She vaguely heard someone saying something about calling the vet.

Felt the presence of people gathering.

Other people crying.

The lady who was driving the car, shoulders shaking, begging for forgiveness.

"I didn't see him, I swear. I didn't see him. It happened so fast..." she sounded frantic.

It didn't look like he was going to make it.

How long until the vet arrived?

She buried her face in his fur. It smelled like grass: pure, sweet green grass.

It smelled like life.

"Charlie please don't die. Please don't leave us. Oh Charlie..."

"I wish you wouldn't die."

The air crackled and her pocket suddenly felt warm.

"Oh my God!" her heart filled with dread as her head snapped up, her hand flying to her mouth.

"I didn't mean it. Please, it was just me thinking out loud. Please..."

Thoughts of tsunami waves and dead bodies flashed through her mind. Images in slow motion, like a silent film, grainy and jerky.

Dread reached her very soul.

Charlie sat up, licked her face, wriggled out of her grasp, ran around in circles and went after the ball.

Jeremy followed, his tears forgotten.

There didn't even seem to be as much blood now.

Where did all the blood go?

A collective sigh of relief went up from the bystanders.

"It's a miracle!" said the postman.

"I've never seen anything like it." exclaimed the neighbor from across the street.

Liz didn't quite catch what everyone was saying. She just sat there stunned.

Jeremy was positively beaming.
Only Liz wasn't.
She was scared.
Reaching into her pocket.
Only one pebble left.
What had she done?

***

Seconds ticked by.
Perhaps even a whole minute, maybe two.
And then she heard it.
"Somebody help me please!" It was Mrs. Mason next door.
"Please! Someone come help me!"
Her second cry sounded even more desperate.
Everyone ran towards her house. There was more screaming. Something unintelligible and a low guttural growl.
Liz ran as fast as she could, pushing her way towards the front of the crowd.
Trixie – Mrs. Mason's chocolate lab was lying on the floor.
Convulsing, foam coming from her mouth.
Round and round her body went on the floor, legs kicking – as if she was trying to run somewhere.
And the sound she was making!
Was that a sound of pain?
Or terror?
Perhaps both.
Suddenly the vet was there.
Where did he come from?
Oh yeah, Charlie, someone had called him for Charlie.
In what seemed to be an agonizingly long time, but was really less than two minutes, Trixie finally stopped convulsing.
Everything was still except for the sound of sniffles.
A hush had come over the bystanders.
The vet examined her.
His face was grim.

And then he confirmed all of their suspicions with a simple shake of his head.

Trixie was no longer with them.

Mrs. Mason collapsed on the floor, heartbroken.

Liz sank beside her, completely and utterly depleted.

Jeremy and Charlie were still outside playing ball, oblivious to the events in the house.

All was right in their world.

***

One of the other neighbors offered to stay with Mrs. Mason until her daughter could make it in the next day from two states away.

Speculation began immediately.

Did she ingest something she shouldn't have?

Perhaps she had an aneurysm?

The vet did a necropsy to no avail. Internal organs were examined and submitted for analysis.

No cause of death was found.

Tissue and fluid examinations were performed. Every test run.

Again, a big fat nothing.

A thousand dollars later – and still no answers

But Liz knew, or at least she was pretty sure she did.

But remember this – every time you make a wish, and are granted that wish, the exact opposite will happen somewhere else.

***

After about a week, the gossip died down.

Some of the men dug a modest grave in the back yard.

There wasn't a lot of fanfare, but someone said a little prayer.

Mrs. Mason was seventy-eight years old and lived alone.

Trixie was only six years old, and had been the love of her life.

What was she going to do now?

It is said dogs live in the here and now, which is good because tomorrow is always a scary place for an older person.

Hell, she'd lost Daniel. Tomorrow's not even a sure thing for the young.

Mrs. Mason didn't have anything to keep her mind off tomorrow now.

Liz found herself spending a lot of time with Mrs. Mason. Trying to make up for something?

Perhaps.

"I never felt alone when she was here. I feel so alone now."

"Maybe you should get another dog?" Liz had suggested hopefully.

"I'm too old for another one, honey. How would I keep up with a puppy?"

And so their conversations went.

A few weeks went by, and Mrs. Mason stopped answering her door.

And her phone.

Once in a while, Liz would see her sitting on the front porch, and would wave, but the older woman seldom appeared to notice anymore.

Liz gave up, but still felt an incredible amount of guilt every time she saw her.

Then she was moved to a nursing home.

Diagnosed with Alzheimer's, at least that was the rumor.

The house sat vacant.

Some people said they heard a low guttural growl coming from inside late at night from time to time.

Liz didn't want to think about it.

She placed the last pebble in her jewelry box – the ghul did say it had to be in her possession, right?

And she was very careful to never, ever say the words "I wish."

***

It was the beginning of August, and Jeremy was turning five.

Where had the time gone?

She remembered it like yesterday when she'd found out

she was pregnant.

The worst and best day of her life.

***

The white light was so bright.

Brighter.

Followed by the horrible crushing sound of metal on metal...

She heard herself scream.

"Mrs. Dodd, I am going to need you to hold still!" The voice issued a firm command.

"Daniel! Where's Daniel?!"

Liz couldn't catch her breath. She knew.

She could feel it in her soul. She felt his loss, even if no one would tell her.

"Mrs. Dodd, I really must insist. If you are going to keep flailing around, I am going to have to sedate you."

"Please... please tell me where Daniel is."

"He's being attended to by someone else. I really can't tell much from over here..."

An obvious lie.

"Now, do I have to sedate you, or are you going to behave and let me get you to the hospital?"

After that, everything was a blur.

She vaguely remembered doctors and nurses coming and going.

The sweet nurse with the soft voice who kept telling her it was going to be okay.

Her mom and dad sitting by her side.

Patting her hand while sipping coffee.

Muffled conversations she couldn't quite focus on.

And then clarity, coming a few days later.

The confirmation of what she already knew.

Daniel hadn't made it.

"Do you understand what I am telling you?"

Liz looked at the spectacled doctor, and nodded.

Yes, she understood.

"Liz, I'm going to release you tomorrow, but I want you

to let your parents take care of you. Your body has been through a lot. You are very lucky to have gotten out of this with only bruises and broken ribs."

"And the baby is fine. That is truly the biggest miracle in all this."

Her mom was smiling at her with tear filled eyes, nodding. "Yes," she whispered softly. "We are so grateful."

Wait, did he say...

Baby?

"I didn't lose my baby?" Liz felt like she was in a fog.

Where was the clarity of a few moments ago?

"You are about five months pregnant. With a boy. You didn't know?"

Know?

It all made sense now.

She thought she had the flu.

Couldn't seem to keep anything down.

Daniel had started to joke that maybe she was *pregnant*.

Oh. My. God.

She was pregnant!

With Daniel's child!

"No." she choked out. "I didn't know"

A baby, a part of Daniel growing inside her.

Tears streamed down her face. It truly was a miracle.

***

Shaking herself out of her thoughts, Liz decided to have a party.

Why not?

Five was a pretty big deal.

You get to put that thumb up and everything.

Besides, there had been too much sadness and stress over the past few months.

And if you're going to throw your son a party, you may as well do it up right.

At least that was Liz's motto.

She rented out the local pool's party area, and arranged for pizza and soda.

Every five year old's dream, right? Even the adults could join in on the fun.

They played Pin the Tail on the Donkey, Hot Potato and Clothespin Drop.

Jeremy absolutely adored the Teenage Mutant Ninja Turtles. So Liz felt like the best mom in the world when she managed to find a local party store that offered costumed characters.

"Michelangelo" was a pretty convincing superhero, even if Liz did see *her* without the costume head.

All the kids totally bought it though. They were especially impressed with his, or rather her, dual nun chuck skills.

There was a mound of presents and Jeremy remembered to say thank you to everyone.

It was a glorious day.

At least until someone decided a game of water chicken was in order.

Kids started pairing off with their dads.

Liz saw Jeremy headed her way.

Everyone started shouting at once.

"Come on Jeremy!"

"Go get your dad and let's go!" a young voice yelled.

"Stupid. Everyone knows he doesn't have a dad," his friend Ryan said.

Ryan's mom quickly grabbed her son's arm and placed her hand over his mouth.

"I'm sorry," she mouthed silently to Liz, looking stricken.

Gasps and an awkward silence followed.

Jeremy stopped running towards her in mid stride and looked around.

It was perhaps the first time he fully realized the implication of those words.

Liz had tried to explain it to him as gently as she could several times. She had showed him Daniel's picture often, making sure he knew what he looked like. She had told him what a wonderful man he was, and that he would have loved to have been a daddy.

Was it possible he never comprehended what she had tried to tell him?

Her dad quickly stepped in.

"Come on Jeremy, You and I are going to win this fight!" He said tugging Jeremy towards the water.

Liz didn't realize she'd been holding her breath until a huge sigh of relief escaped her lips when Jeremy smiled up at his pap, and followed him.

Nothing more was mentioned about his dad, and everything seemed to have been forgotten.

***

Later that evening as Jeremy was getting his bath, Liz noticed his quiet demeanor.

"Mama…?"

"Yes, my love?"

"What does dead mean?"

She watched him draw a star on the tile with his new soap crayons and pondered just what to say.

"Well, dead means a person or an animal stops breathing and are no longer here with us."

"Did Daddy die?"

"Yes Jeremy, Daddy died before you were born."

"Are you going to die?"

This was harder than she imagined.

"Yes, someday I will die."

"Am I going to die?"

"One day baby, yes, you will die."

"Tomorrow?"

"I don't think it will be tomorrow, but no one knows when you are going to die."

"Mama," he said as he climbed out of the tub.

It wasn't really a question so she waited.

"I wish I had a daddy."

"I know baby, I know…"

Wrapping him in a towel, and gently moving him towards his room, Liz felt hot tears stinging her face.

How could she explain to a five year old just how unfair

life could be?

Hell, she didn't even understand it herself.

***

Laying in her room, she thought about the day's events, the past few months, and even the past five years.

Why should Jeremy be without a daddy?

Why should she be without her husband?

Why did all the bad people in the world seem to have or get everything they wanted?

How many people secretly wished their spouse was dead? Or at the very least – gone from their lives.

What would happen if things were different?

What could be the harm?

Sighing, she got up and crossed the room to her jewelry box.

Lifting the lid, she picked up the remaining tiny pebble.

Turning it over and over between her fingers. It felt right, inviting.

But remember this – every time you make a wish, and are granted that wish, the exact opposite will happen somewhere else.

The rain.

Charlie.

She silently wished she had never met that little tiny man.

But maybe…

…Daniel.

Through her tears, she stood in the doorway and watched Jeremy sleeping, as Charlie wandered around her legs.

"I wish…"

The air crackled and her hand suddenly felt very warm.

About Bobbi

Bobbi Carol has an intense fear of writing bios – especially short ones that need to fit on a single page in a book.

She could tell you about her obsession with the color pink – or how she hates the thought of being abducted by aliens – but is that really what the reader wants to know?

She has published some articles on Hub Pages, is the coordinator and editor of two newsletters in the central Pennsylvania area, and also adores her work as a proofreader for Tirgearr Publishing. She does want to mention her day job with the Pennsylvania Statewide Adoption and Permanency Network (SWAN).

She'd like to think she's a budding author with dark thriller tendencies, and even some dystopian sci-fi leanings. But since this is her first published short story, the verdict is still out on her writing style. Some have even dared call her "edgy," but she thinks that just means she might need to switch to decaf.

But in the end – the one and only thing you truly need to know about her? No matter what the question might be – the answer is always ice cream…ALWAYS.

MULTIPLIER

A RIDGE FALLS STORY

Troy Lambert

Surrounded by darkness.

The cellar smelled of old potatoes.

But most cellars in Idaho did, especially those near a reservoir. Dampness invaded every inch.

"Do you have it?" he called down.

"Not yet!" It was hard for the young man to see down here. The darkness was different. Thicker.

He was surrounded. Not just by jars of garden tomatoes long ago forgotten, sitting next to jams and jellies.

Wooden boxes and hope chests sat, some open, some closed. The Reverend said he could have them all, if he brought him only one thing.

A lamp. A tiny, ancient looking, bronze lamp. The Reverend had shown the young man pictures. When he asked him why he couldn't get it himself, the pastor shrugged.

"I am old," he told him. "Damp cellars are for the young."

How could he argue? Reverend Freelander has been the pastor of Ridge Falls Baptist Church for five years. A request from him was like a request from God. Especially when this pastor caught a certain young man stealing from the collection plate, and promised to not tell his parents if he would do this task.

Then he was in, sitting next to a ring, a watch, and a pile of what appeared to be rubies. He wouldn't be able to pawn these locally, or all at once. He'd need to go to Boise, or even further. Maybe Salt Lake now and then.

"I found it," he called out.

"Bring it to me!" the Reverend cried. He heard the excitement in his voice. The anticipation.

"You promise all the rest is mine?"

"I promise. Bring it to me, boy!"

Ferris Wilson grabbed the ring, and slipped it onto his finger. It fit perfectly. He put the watch on his arm. It was clearly an antique piece, with ancient scroll work on the band with a feminine feel, clearly dating back to the time when these were known as arm clocks, and men carried timepieces in their pockets.

Perfect. Sometimes it paid to be young and skinny.

"Hurry!" the Reverend yelled, his voice cracking.

Rushing to the ladder, he saw the white face staring down at him, sweat glistening on his brow, dripping onto the lenses of his gold-rimmed spectacles.

"Give it to me," he said, holding out his hand.

"Not until I am out," Ferris declared.

"Give it to me first."

He sensed something was wrong. There were red splotches high on the pastor's cheeks. The Reverend was breathing faster than he'd have ever heard him do, even in the heat of a sermon.

"No. When I am out."

"Give it to me first, or I'll lock you in."

"Fine," he said, hiding his fear.

The Reverend shocked him then. He turned, looked up at the sky, and howled with anger.

"You will change your mind, boy."

The cellar door closed, and he was left in darkness.

Curious, he turned the weakening beam of his flashlight

to the lamp. Something was inscribed on the side.

Shaking it, he heard liquid slosh. He saw a tiny, protruding wick.

He found a book of matches in his pocket. Maverick Country Stores, it said on the side. Inside, two lone soldiers stood, heads erect, awaiting his bidding. He pulled one from his place, and folded the cover over.

Strike one. So the umpire might have said.

Sparks flew. Flame formed and died.

Fading light from dying batteries.

One more soldier, one more strike. Flame, again.

Please, I hate the dark, he thought.

Struck, caught. Put to the wick.

A giant flame erupted, and shot toward the ceiling. He had no fear of it in this damp space, but it startled him, and he dropped the lamp to the floor.

The flames took shape, forming into a figure of sorts.

"Who are you?" the figure asked.

"I am Ferris. Ferris Wilson." he answered. His legs trembled. He was talking to an apparition.

"I am the genie of the lamp. You are now my master. What do you wish?"

A young Ferris Wilson had no idea what to say, but he knew, as a young man in Ridge Falls, Idaho, what he wanted.

"Power," he answered.

"We will be great friends," the genie declared. If a figure, formed of flame, could grin, he did. "Tell me, what sort of power do you seek?"

THE SEVEN

Ten Years Later

"Your horse is leaving the barn your highness."
"What?"
"Your highness, your…" He points
Damn it. I fumble with my zipper.

Zipper? I'd worn pants with a zipper here? How stupid could I be?

The page stares at my crotch as I fiddle with the metal device I am sure he's never seen before. Hazards of time travel in the wrong pants. And what if it broke? Then what?

My horse would be leaving the barn for a lengthy jaunt then. With effort and concerned care, I manage to secure the enclosure. The page is no longer the only one staring. Suddenly I have an audience.

"My lord…" I know he is going to ask, but then horns sound.

My hand remains in a strategic location apparently concerned with checking its work and smoothing my rough jeans to hide the metal teeth no one in this time had seen, and that surely raised concern in the mind of every man in the room. I look up and note the arrival of the princess. I rapidly move my hand to the side, but not without glancing downward to ensure the concealment of the errant fastener. It must look as amusing and embarrassing as it felt, for the page suppresses a giggle.

"Is everything right my lord?" The musical notes of the princess' voice send my heart into a rapid jig. Her clothing is clearly authentic to the place and period, and though I still have no understanding of how she manages to breathe in the corset and girdles she wears, they accentuate her luscious curves and light a fire in the barn I have only just managed to close.

Were she to discover the truth of my origins, our young marriage would certainly be in jeopardy. She accepts my running off at all times to this country and that, and never attempts to hold me back. There is only one in this time who knows my true identity and how I manage to travel from time to time and world to world.

I value this place above all the rest, not due to its desirable culture, exciting nightlife, and mythical creatures to kill with my sword. I love it above all the rest because she is here, and therefore this is where my heart resides.

"My lord?" she asks again, and I realize I must have been staring off into space.

"Yes my love, everything is right. Especially now that you are here." She moves forward quickly but with perfect posture and grace, her royalty never faltering. I hold out my hand.

She bends and we kiss chastely, but the warmth of her lips promises more to come. "It is good to have you home."

"Yes it is!" comes another voice. I look up to see the enchanter, Freelander, standing in the doorway. Steel fills my belly, and the raging stallion of my passion retreats to the furthest stall in the rear of the barn. For him to come to me this soon after my arrival means trouble, and it means postponing my reunion with my bride and my love.

"Greetings my friend!" I rise with my princess by my side to greet the man I hate most of all, but who also makes my rule of this kingdom and therefore my connection with the woman I love possible. "What news of the Kingdom?"

"There is much to tell, my lord," he says, bowing deeply. "Come, share with me your travels."

I squeeze the hand of the woman I love, then release it to follow him to my private chambers. As I do, we shared a glance, one that promises she too, will visit my chamber when my business is concluded, and unleash the wild stallion from his enclosure.

***

"Show it to me," he says when we were alone. "And what are you wearing?"

"I neglected to change."

"You were visiting our home world." He states it as a fact, leaving no room for argument.

"I have told you, this is my home world," I respond. "That is my world of origin."

"Believe whatever fable you wish, young highness. Now show it to me."

Given no alternative, I remove the object he seeks from the long middle pocket of my tunic. The lamp feels tiny in my hand, as it always has.

He tries to snatch it away, but before he can, I tuck it back into my pocket.

"Fine. I will use other means to divine where and when you have been. Go change to more appropriate attire before this evening."

"This evening?"

"Yes my lord. There is a banquet to celebrate your return."

"Why?"

"The people need reassurance."

"Reassurance? Of what?"

"Your ability to rule," Freelander said, his teeth revealed in a grin contrasting to what felt like bad news.

"Why would they doubt that?" I ask.

"Riders, from the North. I am afraid your stay this time will be short. We need more weapons."

It is the last thing I want to hear him say. Everything I have read, everything in my whole being tells me that bringing things from my world, providing them to this man and my armies means I will change the balance of power, the history forever in this time-stream of events. There may be other consequences I cannot even fathom. But if I do not, and my kingdom is overrun, the enemy will seek to kill me.

If that happens, I won't be able to return.

And she is here. Unlike me, she cannot travel.

The former Reverend Freelander taught me to use the lamp to move things, bring them here. It is, after all, its purpose. But I can't transport living beings. A fly who once clung to my tunic, a rat caught in a box of grenades, both died in the process.

My love cannot come with me. Therefore, I have to do the bidding of this man, and protect the kingdom at all costs.

"They have improved their armor." He interrupts my thoughts. "We need something stronger than the simple weapons you have so far provided."

"Like what?"

He pulls out a wrinkled magazine. I still remember the day I stuck it in my pocket, and brought it here in error. I see the title: "Military Weapons of the West."

"One of these would do nicely," he points. His finger trembles when he touches the glossy pages. Paper. A material so rare here, and so abundant and wasted where I come from.

"Rockets," he says. "We will need at least a dozen."

I stare, wondering how I will find and deliver such weapons. Yet deep down, I already know.

My father. In my world. This order will be no problem at all.

"Give me tonight," I say. "I will go tomorrow."

He wants the lamp itself. Without it, he cannot travel. This is his home, his world, and here he must remain.

I want to stay, but until I satisfy him, I cannot. He will betray me. Unless I keep supplying him with what he wants, a bit at a time. Or I give him the lamp.

With it he would unleash hell here. That I cannot risk.

"Prepare, then Highness. Your subjects await. If you don't mind my saying so, you are in need of bathing."

***

The ballroom is filled with the flickering light of torches and the smell of oil lamps. I've always liked this better than the harsh fluorescents and incandescent bulbs of my home world. The food, strange at first, is delightful once one's palette adjusts.

The women are voluptuous and full bodied. The skinny ones are ridiculed, although I discourage such nonsense. Coming from a society where the opposite is true, I see the argument differently.

If anything, these are the most valuable lessons of visiting time after time, place after place. People are people. Food is food.

And thankfully, ale is ale. The ale here is better and stronger than most. With the enchanter's request, and my love by my side, yet at the moment untouchable, I really want to consume large amounts. But I cannot return to my world, and my father, intoxicated or hung over.

His stash of weapons will be well guarded. He has already become suspicious, even though the amount I have taken so far is so small, you'd think he'd hardly notice. But the man inventories paper clips and pushpins. I have been able to get away with it because the items just disappear. There is no evidence, and he would never suspect me, who he calls his pacifist, hippie son. He suspects his men. That I can live with.

Music swells from the stage, a mix of drum and lyre that until I came here, I never could have imagined.

"Let's dance," she says quietly at my elbow, knowing it is inappropriate for her to ask. That is something I should do.

But she knows I pay little attention to the rules. "Of course," I whisper.

Taking her hand, I lead her to the wide open space near the front of the hall. She moves close to me, and my stallion, heretofore quiet, awakens from his slumber.

"What is on your mind, my lord?" she says, our conversation hidden by the music. Her grin is mischievous as she rubs her thigh against me to verify what she already knows.

"You know, my lady," I say. "But alas, it is not to be."

"Why not?" she says, rubbing harder, teasing.

"Riders come from the North, so Freelander says."

"That enchanter is a fool."

"And yet, if the kingdom is in danger…"

"Will you bring more strange weapons?" Red has risen in her cheeks. Her body is no longer soft and supple, but stiff and unyielding.

"I must."

"What hold does he have on you, that you must do his bidding rather than mine?"

"I have told you before. I cannot explain."

Our pretense of dancing stops. Her hands fall from my shoulders to her hips. "Then tonight, you will sleep alone."

She stomps once, a sign of her defiance, and disappears into the crowd.

"She appears angry. What did you say to her?" the voice in my ear holds more menace than concern.

"Nothing of importance. She wishes me to stay tonight."

"And bed her, no doubt."

"That is none of your concern!" I spin to find the enchanter's face only inches from mine.

"Oh, but it is my lord. Don't delude yourself that I do not know your reason for loving this world."

I stare back at him, but he does not back down.

"You might as well retire to your chambers, my lord. Change into your clothing, the trousers with teeth you wore this morning, and get traveling. The enemy is but a day's journey away."

With all the dignity I can muster, I move through the crowd, nodding and bowing in return to those who nod and bow to me. Honoring my position.

I'm liked for all I have done for the kingdom. After all, my odd weapons have brought a kind of peace, at least for my people.

I cannot speak for the rest of this world. With one last look across the festival filled room, I spot her. Frowning, arms folded, she scowls at me, promising this time, for this going against her wishes, I will surely pay.

Reluctantly excusing my departure, I head to my chamber, but not the one upstairs. The one on the ground floor.

That is an error one only makes once in time travel.

The sooner I go, the sooner I can return.

***

The warehouse is dark, but I dare not use a light of any kind. It's okay, I know how to find what I am looking for. Insanely, the weapons are alphabetized by row. Rockets will be found under R.

Slipping the lamp into my tunic, I stand still for a moment, listening.

The lamp and the arm clock work together. I'm not sure how. I touch the watch to the lamp, and the genie, who typically remains hidden inside, or dwells elsewhere, in some other dimension for all I know, does the rest.

This is why I stand, silent, listening. Time travel, at least this type of time travel, is almost silent. Assuming there are other types. If there are, I don't yet know of them. But each time I appear somewhere, there are two audible pops.

Pop, pop.

The darkness remains dark. The silence rests undisturbed.

I'm not sure how I control where I appear in the whens I travel to, but if I have been there before, and think of a certain place, that's where I arrive. If not, I assume the "landing site" is random. It feels like magic. I prefer to refer to it as undiscovered science.

Row A: Anti-aircraft, anti-personnel.

B: bombs and bullets. What else would be there?

C: CS gas and cyanide.

Cyanide? I suppose it falls into the class of weapon.

There are other objects. Other options. At least one item for nearly every letter in the alphabet. Most I have never heard of. I'd never aspired to, or studied the family business.

P: Heavy boxes, labeled with Pu, and a familiar yellow and black symbol. High school chemistry. Plutonium?

Q: I thought this section would be empty. But there is a small box. Curious, I look inside, and see a half a dozen even smaller boxes. Each is labeled "Quark Multiplier."

With no idea why, or what such a device might do, or be, I take one. It's held closed by a simple clasp, one similar to those that contain the bulging contents of enormous women's purses, the ones that look like they hold a seven-day survival kit, complete with a kitchen sink.

Opening it, I see an instruction book.

Before I can read it, the silence is broken. The beams of two flashlights criss-cross the area where I entered, and two voices rise with excitement. Somehow, I have drawn attention, perhaps tripped an alarm.

I step to the next area, and find two boxes marked simply "Rockets." They are too heavy for me to fully lift, so I simply sit on them. The voices and the lights are getting closer, at least to "M" by now. I pull the lamp out of my pocket, and slip the quark multiplier into its place. I think of the palace, touch the watch to the lamp, and disappear.

A moment later, I hear two pops, and I am in my ground floor chamber, sitting on the two wooden boxes. Less than a minute later, the enchanter bursts through the door.

"Ah, there you are. I was beginning to worry. I see you have acquired what we need."

I find I can't speak. Suddenly, the quark multiplier feels heavy in my tunic. An urge tugs at me, an urge not to tell Freelander about it, and hide it. Right away.

"Well?" he says. "Cat got your tongue? Get off those boxes. Get changed. Perhaps your love will forgive you, and grace your bed after all this evening."

I step off the boxes without a word. Without thinking, or even realizing what I am doing, I touch the watch to the lamp. I'm not even sure where or when I am thinking of.

The enchanter reaches for me, but I somehow know I will reappear before he can track me, object to what I am doing.

What am I doing?

I don't know.

Pop, pop.

The sign is right in front of me: Welcome to Ridge Falls, established 1894. Moved 1944. Back to the odd town where I grew up, retrieved the lamp for him in the first place. The one where my father has hidden his warehouse, and all the arms he sells.

I am on the outskirts, and the edge of the reservoir is only one hundred yards away. Without deciding to, I walk toward the shore and take the odd device from my pocket, sliding the lamp into its place.

Opening the box reveals a strange device with a vial on the side resembling a test tube. I pull it free with practiced ease, as if I have done it a thousand times.

When I reach the shore, I kneel, and fill the vial with water from the man-made lake.

Without thought, I fix the tube back into place on the device, and slide it back into its carrier. It feels lighter somehow.

Removing the lamp, I touch it to the watch, hear the familiar double pop, and I am back in my chamber, in the world I have claimed as my own.

My room is empty. The rockets and Freelander are gone, but suddenly I am not worried at all.

In fact, I am exhausted. Inexplicably so.

With no desire to spend the night here, I make my way to my upstairs chamber. Removing the strange device, I put it and the lamp behind the loose stone near the head of my bed. Without undressing, I fall onto the mattress, and sleep without dreams.

***

Someone is shaking my shoulder.

I mumble for them to stop.

After all, I am the prince. And I am sleeping.

"Get up!" Freelander's voice.

"By the gods, no! Let me be!" I hiss, trying to be both authoritative and quiet out of courtesy to my pounding head. Traveling with the lamp always does that to me.

I feel myself lifted, then sitting on the side of my bed. His face is inches from mine, but blocks the light. For that I am grateful, but his visage is twisted in rage.

"You went back to your world again. Why?" he demands. "You are not to travel without telling me."

"There is nothing to say I must," I answer, knowing I am

being foolish.

"Nothing other than your word, offered in exchange for my continued silence."

"Give me a moment to wake," I say.

"Where did you go last evening so quickly?" he presses again.

"Home, to spend a few moments on the edge of the lake." It is not untrue. Though he says he can trace where and when I go, he cannot see what I did.

Something felt odd about my trip the night before. True, I had gone home, and lingered on the shore of the lake, but the "when" had felt different. The lake felt somehow younger.

The thought seemed right, but made no sense.

"May I have a moment to myself?" I ask. "I find when I rise suddenly, especially after traveling, certain needs take priority."

"Certainly," he said with sarcasm.

"I'll see you at breakfast shortly."

He bows, and leaves, but not without clear trepidation. "Do not try anything foolish," he admonishes.

But he knows I won't. I am in my second floor chamber, twenty feet above the ground. After tending to my needs, I dress before returning to the loose stone, and remove it. It is then I see the odd device, and remember.

A quark multiplier, whatever that may be. A tube on the side, now filled with lake water. I slip the lamp into my pocket, and study the device.

There are no knobs or levers visible. Just a single push button. The water looks odd, gray and murky. As I study it, a few small bubbles appear, moving from the bottom to the top. Slipping it back behind the stone, I head down the stairs, hoping by now my love may have forgiven me.

And to hear news of the riders from the North. At all costs, I must protect my kingdom.

My Kingdom. It sounds odd. This is not my world, and I am told by Freelander that these beings, even the love of my life, are not entirely human. But I feel as if I belong here, and the other places I visit, even the world on which I was born are places where I trespass occasionally.

Touching the walls as I descend the narrow stairway, I feel the warmth of the stone. It remains that way, even in the heart of winter. Idly I wonder why.

***

She sits at the table, and smiles at my appearance, something I take as a good sign. A sign, perhaps, of hope.

Fresh milk awaits, along with fresh eggs, much larger than those I grew up with. A form of sweet bread, similar to a doughnut but far more delicate and delectable sits at my place. A citrus juice similar, but slightly more tart than orange juice has been poured.

I do little for myself here. I have servants who perform every task, and I have been told I could demand more, and do even less if I so desired. I do not. I like to be active, and feel better when I am moving, doing things on my own.

But others doing the cooking is one thing I do enjoy.

"My lord," she greets me, and her and the enchanter rise.

"Sit," I say. "I trust you slept well?"

"I did. But I missed your presence in my chamber. Perhaps later we could discuss arrangements for this evening."

"Indeed," I say with a smile. When it was returned with all of her features except her eyes, I replace my hope with caution. All was not yet forgiven.

Searching the table and coming up empty, I ask, "There is no coffee this morning?"

"No, sire. Since your last absence, we have trouble obtaining it," a servant dressed in kitchen whites states from the door.

"Why is that?"

"The tribes to the West. They refuse to sell it to us or trade, unless we share the new weapons we have *developed*."

Not missing the emphasis on the last word, one I knew most citizens did not believe, I reply, "Are there other

Kingdoms that feel the same?"

"Yes," the enchanter answers for him. "I have been talking to several."

"With what outcome?" From the corner of my eye, I see my bride is frowning. No good can come of this line of questioning, but I must know. I cannot keep taking from my father, and also cannot help but feel it is foolish to escalate an arms race in this otherwise peaceful world.

"We have choices. We can side with one group, the East, the West, even the North, if they will cease hostilities long enough."

"Or?" I say, sensing he is not yet done.

"We can create a great industry, and sell to them all."

"My source is limited," I declare.

"We are not without resources of our own," he answers, glancing at my bride as well. "Perhaps we should discuss this at another time."

He is right. She is seething, and though she knows I travel and bring back strange devices, mostly weapons of late, she does not know where I go. Or rather, when.

This is all so confusing. And I want it to stop.

"Excuse me," the enchanter says abruptly. "I will check on the skirmish in the North, and inform you of progress later this morning."

Spinning on his heel, he heads for the door. When he is gone, and the servant has cleared the first round of dishes, my bride turns on me.

"I told you this would come to no good. Where do you get the weapons anyway?"

"You know I cannot say."

"Cannot or will not?" she snaps. "Do you not trust me?"

"I do, with my very life."

"Then why can you not share this with me?"

I place my head in my hands. I want to tell her, want to confess. But if I do, and Freelander discovers my treachery, he could...

Could what? I ask myself. *Take from me the lamp, so I cannot leave?* There was a time when that might have been a valid threat, but it is no longer. I no longer have a desire to leave, in fact would be quite content to spend the rest of my days here.

But what of the kingdom, and the weapons? They have begun something heretofore unknown here, given my warriors an unfair advantage.

Unless they were all destroyed, and the enchanter could be removed from power. He has some kind of hold over the people here. If I knew what it was, perhaps I could end it.

I look up, and find sympathy yet puzzlement in her gaze.

"Tell me, my love, what do you know of the enchanter, Freelander?"

"Much," she declares. "He came to the kingdom at the invitation of my grandfather."

"Where did he come from?"

"Some say another world. One filled with magic, both good and bad. He has always professed to be on the side of good. But my father had doubts."

"Come, let us go outside. Perhaps we can talk as we walk?"

She catches my meaning. In the courtyard, no one can approach without our knowledge. In the open, we find the privacy we need.

***

"Tell me more," I state, gesturing to a stone bench.

"He is not of our race, and neither are you," she says, sitting.

Startled, I stay standing. "How do you know this?"

"I didn't," she says slyly. "At least of you. I divined it, and you confirmed it just now."

My mouth opens in a giant "O" and I endeavor to close it. Slowly I sink downward and sit.

"I am not as naïve as you believe. The enchanter himself arrived under less than normal circumstances, and himself predicted the arrival of another."

"Predicted?" I wonder aloud. Then I thought back, and

the pieces of the puzzle start to fall into place. "Tell me more, especially of this prophecy of his."

"My grandfather told me of his coming. I don't know if for a warning, or simply because he wanted me to know. He came with another man, one who looked much like you."

"Much like me?"

"That man did not stay. My grandfather said he saw them fighting.

"Fighting?"

"Wrestling over something. Something that appeared to be small, and gold in color."

"What happened?"

"The man who looked like you triumphed, and disappeared. With two loud noises."

I remain silent, but she stares at me, as if expecting me to say something.

"Like the two loud noises that often accompany your return from your journeys."

Still, I remain silent. I want so much to simply tell her.

"The enchanter, as Freelander came to be called, became sullen and foul tempered. He traveled to the other kingdoms, but primarily to the North. Upon his return from one of his journeys, he changed."

"Changed how?"

"He appeared happy. Told my grandfather and the other members of the council that ruled at that time that he would be away, traveling for an extended period. He told them he would come again, with a prince. One who was to be our ruler. Who would take our kingdom to new heights.

"That ruler was you, my Lord. You are the first prince of this kingdom."

"The first?"

"Before your time we were ruled by Councils. All of the kingdoms were. Now, kings or princes rule."

"In the other kingdoms as well?"

"From what we know. There, kings are chosen, not as you were, but from the commoners."

"Why?"

"When they saw that we had a prince, they wanted one as well. When we obtained weapons, they obtained weapons. More than just for hunting food, but for harming each other."

"None existed before me?"

"Crude weapons came with the enchanter. As men began to fight, crude armor formed for defense. Each escalated in proportion to the others. Men began to work metal found in stones and caves beneath the earth into more than just pots and the heads of arrows."

"And when I came?" I said quietly.

"When you came, with you came new weapons. We now rule, not because of superior intellect or morals, but victory in war. Won with weapons you have brought."

"Then why do you love me?"

"You do not do this for yourself. It is Freelander who desires war. Inside, you are a man of peace, but a man conflicted."

"You see all this?"

"I do. But I want so much for you to tell me who you are."

"But…"

"Do not say you cannot. I already know or have discerned more than you thought I did. Tell me who you are, and where you go when you are away."

"I am Ferris Wilson, Junior," I begin. "In my world, that means I am named for my father. I think he was the first to come here. The one who looked like me."

"And where do you go when you leave?" she asked.

"I visit many worlds, but most often, I go home."

"That is where the weapons come from?"

"Yes. A place called Ridge Falls. From a supply my father has."

"Where did he get them?"

"I think I know that now. And I think I know how to put all things right."

"How?"

"I will use the lamp. But, my love, I don't know that I will be able to stay when this is all over."

"So I must choose; you, or peace for my world."

"Perhaps. I do not know."

She sits, unmoving, for several long moments. I stay silent, looking at the courtyard, the walls I want so desperately to stay within.

"I will hope," she says at last.

"Hope for what?" I ask.

"Hope that you can make all right, and still remain here, with me, when all is finished. But if you must choose one or the other…" Her words die out, and she turns to me, holding out both hands.

"Yes?" I say softly.

"Make this right."

I vow to do just that, we embrace, and then kiss.

A few moments later, I part from her, resolved to do what I must.

***

My horse waits. I learned to ride in the mountains of central Idaho, north of my home. There I hunted with a rifle, handed down from my grandfather. We tracked deer and elk, killed and cleaned them, stocked the freezer for winter. The horses carried us into the woods, helped pack out the animals we killed.

I couldn't bring my mount, a gelding oddly named Gary, with me when I transferred here. But as prince, I had been provided one. A fine one, beyond what I would have been able to afford back home. When I was away, he was exercised, and apparently by someone very enthusiastic, for he was always in excellent shape.

And fast.

Today, fast is important.

Because when I had entered the armory, I saw something that chilled my bones. Two boxes marked "rockets", sat empty.

Freelander had ridden out with them and several men. They'd taken a wagon.

So the farrier told me.

A two hour lead was a brilliant head start. But the wagon will slow them. I hope.

In my tunic is the lamp. On my wrist is the arm clock. In another pocket is the quark multiplier, the odd device I brought with me.

As soon as I removed it from its hiding place just moments before, it felt warm to the touch. It feels warmer now.

I hope it will tell me when to use it. And where.

"Hai, Royal! Ride!" I kick my mount into a gallop.

The ride north is not easy. Mountains rise, rocks litter the road, sometimes not much more than a wagon width, pitted with ruts. It is in poor repair.

But we had weapons. That would have to change. Priorities had been skewed, important things neglected. Infrastructure.

Often, I am forced to leave the trail to let others pass by. I can only hope Freelander and the others have to do the same. The people wave, some even bowing. I acknowledge what I must, and push on.

Topping a rise, I see them ahead, near the end of the valley. At first nothing more than a dust trail, they come into focus. I have been riding hard all day without stopping, and my bones are not used to such abuse.

I stop only for a moment, pulling a long swallow of water from my leather flask, and consuming a stick of salty jerky.

In my pocket, the quark multiplier grows ever warmer.

There is no use in trying to disguise my approach. The same open ground that lets me see them, also lets them see me. But they may not know who I am, or why I am coming.

But I think Freelander is smarter than that.

As I watch, the advance of the wagon halts. For a moment, I wonder why.

Then, over the other side of the valley, another column

rises. A large force of men on horseback, the forces of the North, race down the hill to meet them.

There is to be a battle.

I hear the first gunshots, and kick my mount into motion again. We race down the hillside toward the men of my kingdom, far outnumbered, but who outgun the arrows and catapults of the North a hundredfold.

As I watch, men begin to fall from their mounts. From the west comes another column of dust. I can't tell who is attacking whom.

***

Gunshots. Shouts of pain. Still I ride on. Unarmed.

Except for the lamp, and an odd device that gets warmer and warmer until I fear it will set my tunic on fire.

Four hundred yards to chaos. Three.

Two hundred.

One hundred.

Fifty. Something bites me in the shoulder, and I am thrown free of the saddle.

I hit the ground, and roll to my feet. My right arm dangles, weak and nearly useless.

Before me stands Freelander. He raises a weapon.

"You come unarmed to a gun fight? When you are gone, I will be the master of the lamp once more."

Using my left arm, I struggle to pull the odd device free of my pocket. When I touch it, it cools.

He laughs at the gesture. "What? Do you hold the lamp? What good will the genie do you now?"

"It is not the lamp," I say. I feel the pain in my arm, but it seems distant, belonging to someone else.

"Whatever you have, it is too late." He gestures, and my eyes wander. Two men have the rockets on their shoulders, ready to fire. I hear more gunfire, and cries of pain. The cries of war.

The tiny latch defeats my clumsy southpaw, and I struggle to move my right arm to help.

"What is that?" he comes closer.

And then laughs.

"I know what this is! Your father once showed it to me. It will do you no good here."

One moment it is in my hand, the next he is holding the device. He opens the lid.

Turns it toward me.

The water in the tube is black now, seeming to boil. There are things, tiny things in it.

I can see them. Time slows. His finger hovers over the button.

"Here," he declares. "I will show you."

His finger lowers. I hear a small click.

The tube opens, and the water trickles in a small stream onto the ground, forming a tiny wet spot in the sand.

Then nothing.

"You see?' he says. "Nothi—"

The words are torn from this mouth, as a huge wall of water erupts around him in a gigantic wave.

As I watch, it gathers around the group of soldiers, surrounds them. I cannot see clearly through the water, but shadows move in and out, some looking not at all human. Screaming starts, and does not stop.

A hand extends from the wall of water, and is cut off. It drops to the sand, the fingers still moving. It was holding something. The quark multiplier. I grab it, and put it in my tunic without thinking.

The dome of water rapidly shrinks. I hear sounds from inside, sounds like crunching bones. For a moment, the water turns pink, and then goes dark again. Finally, the height diminishes, but it flattens and begins to fill the valley.

I watch as the armies attempt to flee. Those who do not get away fast enough are swallowed by the waves. The newly formed lake appears to grab their horses by the legs, pull them down, and devour both man and beast alike. Those who do reach higher ground turn to watch in fear.

It is only then I see the water is only inches from my boots. I take out the lamp, and rub the side vigorously. A flame instantly forms, and takes on the shape of a man. His head appears to look around.

"Take me from this place!" I shout.

"Where do you want to go?"

"Home," I say, bringing the watch close.

"As you wish."

Two pops sound, and I find myself standing, eyes closed. My arm seems like it is on fire, and I fall forward. My head strikes something hard, and darkness takes over.

***

Water drips onto my head.

I panic, open my eyes, sit up.

White linen surrounds me. A sheer canopy of silk.

Where am I?

Not a hospital. Not Ridge Falls.

The stone gives away the location, before I hear her speak.

"Welcome back, my lord." She grins, and I grin back.

I am still in my tunic, laying on the bed in her chamber. A place I have been many times.

Panicked, I sit up and search my tunic. The Lamp. The odd device. Both are gone.

"Looking for those?" She points to the two objects, resting on a table at the foot of the bed.

"My love, I can explain."

"Later," she says. "But first you must explain these."

She lifts my tunic, and I see I am wearing my rough jeans, the one with the zipper.

Behind the metal teeth, my stallion rises in the barn at her look, and then her touch as she caresses the metal gently with her fingers.

"I have never seen such an enclosure. What is it called?"

"It is a zipper, my lady," I explain. I have nothing to hide any more.

After all, I am home.

About Troy

Author Troy Lambert, recently nominated for the Idaho Statesman's "Best of Treasure Valley" publication as an "Author of the Year", and now an active member of the International Thriller Writers Organization recently released the third and final book in the Samuel Elijah Johnson Series, titled *Confession*, and a collection of short stories titled *Into the Darkness* with Marlie Harris.

Passionate about writing dark, psychological thrillers, his work includes *Broken Bones*, a collection of his short stories, *Redemption*, the first in the Samuel Elijah Johnson Series, *Temptation*, the sequel to Redemption, along with the horror *Satanarium*, co-authored with Poppet and published by Wild Wolf Publishing.

Don't think he lacks diversity as, this year, *Stray Ally* (for dog lovers) was published March 4th by Tirgearr Publishing and an erotic thriller novella, *One Night in Boise*, part of the "City Nights" series also by Tirgearr Publishing, was available as of May 27th.

Mr. Lambert began his writing life at a young age, penning the as yet unpublished *George and the Giant Castle* at age six. He grew up in southern Idaho, and after many adventures including a short stint in the US Army and a diverse education, Troy returned to Boise, Idaho where he works as a freelance writer, analyst, and editor.

Troy lives with his two of his five children and two very talented dogs. He enjoys the outdoors as an active skier, cyclist, hiker, angler, hunter, and a terrible beginning golfer.

Author Website: www.troylambertwrites.com
Twitter: https://twitter.com/authortroy
Facebook: https://www.facebook.com/pages/Troy-Lambert/191932724173411?ref=hl
Amazon Author page: http://www.amazon.com/Troy-Lambert/e/B005LL1QEC
Goodreads: https://www.goodreads.com/Authrotroy
Smashwords:

https://www.smashwords.com/profile/view/AuthorTroy
Linkedin:
http://www.linkedin.com/profile/view?id=106106955&trk=nav_responsive_tab_profile
Pinterest: http://www.pinterest.com/authortroy/

Made in the USA
Charleston, SC
13 March 2015